COMPLETION

Tondrika Hayes

“Even death must die.”

Dedication

This book is dedicated to the numerous people that shaped me into the person I am today. To the people who taught me to be fearless and to embrace my flaws. To those who reminded me to persevere when times were rough and when I lost sight refocused my vision. To my mother for supporting my crazy endeavors. To my sister and cousin for being shining examples of going after the things you want. To my best friends for hounding me until I finished this book and not letting me quit. To Lauren Houtz for dealing with my late-night rambles and helping me give Ky a unique voice.

"There are three types of people that dream..."

Completion

Self-published
thayestheauthor@gmail.com

1

Ice. Her fingers were ice. The stiffened, dead fingers gripped around the notebook in her hand as if her dying breath was spent protecting it from unworthy eyes. She had not died at peace; I could see it in the still gray eyes filled with cataracts and memories that I would never unlock. Her black dreads tinted with hints of gray spilled over the cold steel table like the broken veins of a river, never to return to their source. Her dark wrinkled face was an older reflection of mine staring back at me. I remembered the picture that used to sit on the mantle of the fireplace before my mother took it down. The toothless smile of my aunt's younger self used to gaze back at me as I gazed upon it with my own toothless smile. When I was younger, I was overly conscious about my darker-toned skin, but knowing my aunt looked the same as I gave me some solace.

“I just need you to confirm that it’s her,” the medical examiner whispered as if he was interrupting a conversation.

“Yes. That’s her. How did she die?”

“I’m not sure yet. I’ll know more after the autopsy.”

I nodded and reached out again to place my hand on the cold skin of her arm.

My aunt Sheryl had been what others like to call eccentric. She lived alone in a two-bedroom house tucked into the backwaters of our hometown. I had never visited. I had only been to her home once in a rushed panic with my mother when I was ten. On the car ride out of the woods, my mother made me swear never to go back there again. My mother’s hatred for her sister was something I never entirely understood. It had always been that way, and even my dad hadn’t fully understood its origin. Sometimes I wondered if it was the town and not my aunt that she hated.

The old town had long allowed itself to fall into the guise of an old-timey tourist trap and only a few of the original families had stayed. My mother had always hated living there even when I was of an age that she thought was too young for me to remember the heated arguments she had with my father about moving. Coverton was what tourists would call cozy. The streets and buildings looked like a photo straight out of a 1950s soap ad. Our town's only claim to fame was a bridge that was supposedly haunted. There had never been any real evidence of anything going on at the covered bridge, but underneath someone had strung up a bunch of pill bottles full of trinkets and bits of paper with codes that no one could decipher. I had never bought into the hype until the night right before my high school graduation when a few friends and I took the bridge as a shortcut to get home. As soon as we ducked underneath the decaying planks, a man was standing--

“Do I have your permission?” the medical examiner croaked, awkwardly shifting from one foot to the other.

I jumped but smiled slightly, trying to ease the tension as he stared at me expectantly. For someone that spent their days with dead bodies, I guess being around the living wasn’t an experience he enjoyed.

I gulped, realizing I had no idea what he had asked me, “I’m sorry. What was the question?”

“The um…rigor mortis has set in. I would have to break the fingers to remove the book.”

“Oh.” I frowned, turning back towards my aunt and leaned over the table trying to read the faint writing across the top.

The only things I could make out were the letter L and a seven scratched in Sheryl's careful handwriting. Her fingers, wrapped tightly around the book covered the rest.

"Do I have your permission?" he asked again, the small huff in his voice told me he was getting flustered.

"Yeah. Go ahead," I took a step back to let the man work.

I looked over my shoulder to the equipment on the table: scalpels, tweezers, something that looked like the hose at the dentist's office. Without another word, he moved past me and grasped her fingers tight and pulled. They didn't budge. I looked away and back again as he pulled; a small bead of sweat popped out of his hairline at the effort. A mumbled grunt wheezed past his lips as he closed his eyes and tugged harder.

"I'm going to need a bone saw," he said with finality before stalking off to a cabinet on the other side of the room.

I took my place next to the table again and placed my hand on hers. A momentary warmth replaced the chill of her skin; my breath hitched as the fingers relaxed just enough for me to slip the notebook out. I jerked slightly and pulled away with the book in my hands. A gasp pulled past my lips when her eyes slid shut. Her face visibly relaxed now that the book was in my hands. I looked down to the weathered black composition book in my hands. Across the front in bold black writing was **Life 7: Human 4.**

"How did you do that?" The ME's voice cracked behind me; his eyes were wide in what I guessed was either fear or amazement.

"I don't know. I just touched her hand, and she let go."

I clutched the notebook to my chest, suddenly feeling very protective over the book.

"Oh. Good. I won't have to do as much reconstruction later." He smiled, but I noticed his gaze drifting down to the book in my hands.

"Yeah. Well, I'll let you get to work. I'll tell the funeral home to get in touch with you."

I stuffed the book into my bag, slung the strap over my shoulder and backed out of the morgue. I swore he stared at the bag as I walked away.

Once I stepped out onto the street, I released a breath I didn't realize I was holding. As I walked down the candy strewn sidewalk from the Halloween parade earlier that day, I felt uneasy. Was someone following me? My stomach clenched, and I could feel a cold sweat creeping up my neck. I looked back and ran smack into someone, both of us hitting the unforgiving pavement hard. I reached down to push myself off the ground and stuck my hand in a wad of half-chewed bubble gum.

"Need a hand?" A deep voice broke me out of my disgust as I looked up into the eyes of…

"Trent?"

I groaned as I tried to scrub the blue ball of saliva and sugar onto the pavement. He smiled and brushed the leftover dirt off his clothes before helping me to my feet. For a moment, I couldn't help but stare into the cerulean blue eyes of my ex. But then my eyes fell to the too-tight green leather shirt he was wearing, and I remembered why we broke up.

"It's good to see you, Ky." He lifted my hand to his lips, kissing the small scrape on the palm of my hand.

"I wish I could say the same, Trent." I brushed past him and continued down the sidewalk; the steady fall of footsteps behind me told me he was following.

"Ky, come on. It's been a whole year. Hey—" His hand gripped my shoulder hard, bringing me up short.

I whirled to face him. A steady warmth crept up my neck and into my face. I could feel my hands trembling as they curled into fists at my side. A few people standing in front of the antique shop window tried to subtly turn our direction to see what would unfold.

"Hey, chill. I didn't expect to see you back in town." He smoothed his hand over the dark waves of his hair, "I didn't expect to see you ever again, to be honest."

"I'm only here because my aunt, Sheryl died. I'm making arrangements. I'll be gone by Thursday."

"Oh, man. Sorry to hear that, Ky. If you need anything," he lowered his gaze, "and I mean anything, just let me know."

"Yeah. Thanks." I rolled my eyes and walked the last few feet to my car.

Even as I pulled out of the parking spot, I could still feel his eyes watching me, and I again couldn't shake the feeling that someone aside from my annoying ex was watching me as well.

2

Ten minutes later, I turned down the driveway that led to my childhood home.

Crunch!

"Son of a …" I let the word die on my lips as I heard and felt the gravel from the driveway dent the underside of the car I rented for the weekend.

I stepped out onto the driveway and knelt, running my hand under the car, praying I didn't feel a leak. I snorted, realizing I had no idea what I was doing. Everything seemed to be in place, but I whispered to myself to get an SUV tomorrow. I continued down the driveway slower this time until I parked the car in front of the old shotgun house that had been my childhood home. The cheney berry trees and cactus growing from the rooftop were the same as I had left them, just bigger and slowly reclaiming the house as their own. I fiddled around at the wobbly stump leading up to the brick lain porch, looking for the key my mother had said was buried there. A sudden burst of ants from a slowly forming colony underneath sent me reeling and onto my butt.

"Oh, come on." A groan broke past my lips as I tried to brush the red clay off my jeans and hoodie.

Amidst the anthill was the small clear pill bottle that the key was buried in. I pulled the remainder of the Reese's I had been eating and tossed it to the side of the hill. The ants quickly swarmed it, and I made a mental note to poison the piece of chocolate later. As I pulled the small container from the dirt and stepped up onto the porch, I couldn't help but smile at the memories it brought back. Shucking corn on holidays, snapping peas for money as a kid, and grilling in the front yard on holidays.

I keyed into the house, immediately coughing and sneezing from the dirt that broke free when I opened the door. I had finally convinced my mom to move to Los Angeles with me and forget the old, dilapidated building behind. It had been harder than I expected, considering how much she hated the town and the people in it. To be honest, I wasn't entirely sure if it was safe to be in here, but my mother had said my aunt's will was stashed in a trunk in the living room. My dirt-outlined footprints stood stark against the peel and stick vinyl floor as I looked around through what my mother had left. Most of the chests were filled with clothes and old knick-knacks that had no value except for someone looking to fall into a sentimental tangent. I laughed at the slowly molding collection of comics from my youth. I was glad I outgrew fairytales.

After searching the other rooms in the house, I made my way to my mom's bedroom and found the chest in a corner. The lock had rusted off a long time ago and hung limp against the lid. I opened it carefully, pulled the envelopes out, and began walking back towards the car. I froze when I reached to grab the handle, and it opened smoothly under my fingers.

"I didn't leave the door open, did I?" I whispered and looked around me.

Nothing seemed out of the ordinary. There was just a stray cat watching me from the abandoned house next door, its tail softly sweeping away at the collection of cheney berries on the stoop.

"Did you see anyone near my car, Mr. Cat?" I chuckled to myself.

The cat arched his back as it reared up on all fours, a deep growl and hiss pouring from its lips. His paw reached up and scratched at some invisible force that only he could see. I turned to look in the direction that it was staring but saw nothing. The feeling was back. My mind screamed for me to get in the car and get out of there; I did, leaving the cat and whatever it had seen in my rearview. Gravel bounced hard against the side of the car as I sped down the driveway. When I looked up into the rearview, I would have sworn I saw someone walk around the side of the house, but I quickly dismissed it as paranoia. I turned up the radio of the car, my hand shaking as I reached for the volume knob. The faint sound of a cat yowling momentarily broke through the reverb around me.

"Must have been a stray dog," I stated.

Saying it aloud seemed to make it real.

Later that night, I sank onto the hotel bed. An involuntary sigh pulled past my lips as I shrugged off the hoodie and kicked off my combat boots. I turned to look in the mirror resting above the small dresser in the room. I looked like shit. An exhausted smile broke out on my face as I tried to untangle the mess of my locs.

When I had arrived, they were in a pristine updo that had slowly worked its way loose during the day. I ran a hand through my hair, untangling the locs and letting them fall over my shoulder. The most noticeable thing was the deep circles under my eyes. They were a stark contrast to my normally smooth skintone that my coworkers thought was makeup. I laughed remembering the conversation and how I explained to them the only thing I wore was melanin. The scream of a siren outside broke me out of my musing, and I crossed over the thin bruised-cherry carpet to look out the window and onto the street.

There wasn't much to look at in this town, but the view of a poorly lit main street in backwater Georgia had its charms to tourists. The ambulance, or meat wagon as the locals called it, was parked outside the 24-hour diner down the street from the hotel. A few minutes went by before someone was wheeled out on a stretcher and dumped into the back of the ambulance. Its lights and sirens wailed off into the night toward the hospital. A small crowd had gathered around the outside of the diner. Everyone in this town was so nosy, but I guess I couldn't talk. The commotion had been enough to pull my prying eyes to the window as well. I would have walked the short distance to the diner, but the pull of my head towards my chest reminded me how exhausted I was. After showering and slipping into the tank top and shorts I had brought with me, I slipped underneath the covers and let sleep claim me.

The first thing I noticed upon waking was that I wasn't alone. The slight dip in weight on the bed next to me was what pulled me out of my sleep in the first place. I cracked my eyes open, searching for anything I could use for a weapon. My eyes settled on the paperweight sitting on the nightstand, the thin line of moonlight glinting off its rounded surface. I felt my muscles coil and release as I sprung towards the paperweight, my weight shifting to roll over and bring the paperweight crashing against…

“Trent.” I kept the paperweight posed above my head, ready just in case.

“I’m sorry, Ky. I didn’t know where else to go,” His voice was strained; his hand was clutching his side.

My arm lowered as I noticed the red bubbling through his clasped fingers.

“Oh, my God. You’re bleeding.”

“Well, thanks, Captain Obvious.” He tried to laugh, but a hiss escaped his lips instead.

I reached for my phone, and his hand shot out to grab mine. His grip was strong and made me drop the phone on the bed.

“No doctors. I just need you to stop the bleeding,” he groaned.

“I’m not a doctor. I’m a photographer. You need professional help.”

“No.” His voice was still strained but forceful.

I just nodded and pushed him back onto the bed before grabbing towels from the bathroom. There was no point in arguing with him; his stubbornness was part of the reason we went out separate ways. I gently moved his hand away and pressed one of the towels to his side. His hand covered mine as I pressed hard against the wound. A slow breath pulled past his lips, and his eyes slid shut.

“Don’t close your eyes. You need to stay awake,” I reprimanded.

“That’s for concussions, Little Ms. Yale. I was stabbed,” He grimaced, and a sheen of sweat burst across his lip.

“Stabbed? We need to call the police.” I tried to move, but his grip went back to my arm, keeping me in place.

“No. It's fine. I’m fine. My people are on their way.”

“Your people. What have you dragged me into? I am only here for two more days.”

“Ky.”

“I’m supposed to be planning a funeral, and now I’m keeping you from bleeding out.”

“Ky.”

“Are you in a gang? Are they going to think I’m in the gang too?”

“Ky!”

My head snapped towards him, a weak laugh playing on his lips. Before he could say anything else, I heard the creak of the door and a dark-haired woman that I had never seen before strode into the room. She pushed my hand away, replacing it with her own before helping Trent to stand. He smiled weakly at me as he put an arm around the woman.

"Agent Cortell this is my friend Ky. Ky, this is Agent A…" Trent started.

"Let's keep it to last names. The less she knows, the better. Agent Cortell. I'm with the Bureau," She nodded politely as they walked out the door together.

"Like the Federal Bureau. Like FBI?" I called after them.

They ignored me, but I could make out Agent Cortell saying something about she thought I would be smarter for a Yale grad. Once they left I stared at the bedsheet stained lightly with Trent's blood and the blood-soaked towel on the floor. I picked it up unsure what to do with it and decided to just wrap it up in the plastic bag from my dry cleaning. Then I just sat down at the window with my knees up to my chest. I rubbed my hands over my knees, trying to make sense of what just happened. Was Trent FBI? What was going on? Why was the FBI in town? Does the FBI work like that? What if the housekeeper finds the bloody towel? Doesn't the FBI have people to clean up situations? Does that only happen in movies? I have blood on my hands.

I froze. I still had blood on my hands. Under my nails. A thin dried line running down the length of my finger and across my palm. Another line mixed into the crevice of my lifeline. I slowly rose and walked over to the bathroom and turned on the hot water. Trent's blood swirled pink down the drain, but the residual pink was still there. I grabbed the soap bar the hotel provided and scrubbed turning the once pristine white bar pink.

A. B. C. D. E. F. G.

I scrubbed the bar over my nails, small bits of soap and dried blood flaked into the sink like demented snowflakes.

H. I. J. K. L. MNOP.

The soap was beginning to froth in the sink, a bubbling pink foam, thicker than the froth on a malted strawberry shake gurgled its way down the drain.

Q. R. S. T. U. V.

The water wasn't hot enough. I needed it to be hotter. I needed to burn the DNA from my skin.

W. X. Y. Z. Z. Z. Z.

My eyes lifted to the mirror above the sink. Suddenly I felt ill and shaky. I reached for the door to steady myself but slipped to the floor darkness taking over.

3

That's cold.

The thought ripped through my mind as my eyes snapped open again. Instead of the floor, I was lying on the bed. The cloth that had been on my forehead moments before fell into my lap forgotten as I stared into the faces of Trent, Agent Cortell and a larger man that I hadn't met.

"Don't scream," Trent smiled.

"I'm not a walking cliché." I pushed myself to sit back against the headboard.

"Easy. Adrenaline is a hell of a drug, but the crash is terrible." Trent placed his hand lightly on my leg.

"She's taking this surprisingly well," the man whispered to Agent Cortell.

Cortell rolled her eyes and came to sit on the other side of me. She roughly pulled my arm to her and placed her fingers on my wrist as if checking my pulse.

"It's normal again. She's okay we can go now," she huffed.

"Not until I explain what I can," Trent shot over his shoulder.

Cortell seemed taken aback for a moment but stepped away regardless. She motioned for the other guy to follow her out the door.

"Three minutes," she said as she eased the door closed behind them.

For a moment we just stared at each other.

"How's the side?" I cleared my throat.

"That's the question you ask," Trent laughs.

"I've watched enough TV drama to know not to ask too many questions."

"Okay. Well, allow me. Um…let's see. I'm FBI now. I'm working undercover."

I nodded and forced myself to say nothing.

"No response yet. Okay. The case I'm working is trying to infiltrate a cult that the government believes has settled here in Coverton."

"Mmmhmmm. Right. Cult. Got it."

"Ky, you always were special," he smiled slightly before continuing "yesterday when I saw you I was shocked because I never expected to see you back here and then you said your Aunt Sheryl died and I was concerned, so I followed you."

"So someone was following me when I went home."

"Yeah. I had to be sure."

"Sure of what?"

"That you weren't a part of the cult."

“Why? How would I be a part of a cult? I haven’t been back here in 2 years.”

“Because we have reason to believe your aunt Sheryl was their leader.”

I froze. A strange pressure seemed to take purchase in my throat. Was that the reason my mother had warned me to stay away from her?

“Ky? Did you hear me?”

“What?”

“I said, did you find anything strange in your aunt’s belongings so far?”

“Unusual? No.” My mind drifted to the notebook Sheryl had died holding.

“You sure. It seemed like you were thinking about something for a second there.”

“Yeah. Um…nothing unusual just a diary about how she planted her garden.”

I don't know why I lied but I felt like I should, considering I hadn't even opened the book myself. His gaze bore into mine, and I did my best to keep my breathing steady and not look to the left. Or was is the right that people look to when they're guilty.

"If you find anything you'll let me know right," He said, taking my hand in his.

"Of course." The familiar tingle shot up my spine at his touch. I cleared my throat as he pulled away. He stood up and walked towards the door.

"Wait. I have a question. How did you get stabbed?"

"Oh that. Bar fight. Unrelated to work." He threw a smile over his shoulder before closing the door behind him.

After a moment, I rushed into the bathroom to check for the bloody towels, but they were gone. I sighed in relief, that was one thing I didn't have to worry about. Now for the book. I reached for the bookbag that I had discarded the night before and pulled the weathered notebook from the zipped compartment in the back. For some reason I felt the need to lock the door and pull the curtains closed before sinking into the hard recliner next to the window. I reached over to turn on the small lamp on the table and ran my fingers over the book. The first thing I noticed upon opening the book was the folded note written on what appeared to be parchment paper. I sat the notebook aside and carefully unfolded the paper. The edges were all covered with symbols that looked like a mixture of letters and a first-grade artist's idea of what animals looked like, but in the middle was a letter addressed to me.

Kyhlia,

If you are reading this, then I am dead. My niece I wrote you this letter in the hopes that you

will continue the work that I have already started. It will all seem very confusing at first and without me there to protect you there is a possibility that other forces may be after you already. My dear niece, the knowledge contained in this notebook and those before it is lofty, and I understand if you do not want to undertake my task. Know that once you have begun reading there is no turning back. I do not write this to trick you into reading for the sake of curiosity. This is meant solely as a warning. If you decide to take on this task you will always be in danger, and there will be some days that you will feel alone in this world. You may have to abandon your family and friends to protect this secret. There are seven notebooks total. The other six are in my home for you to find. Read them in order saving this one for last. If you choose not to accept this task I ask that you unload the burden onto someone you

trust that will be strong. I love you Kyhlia. I wish I could have properly trained you for what is to come. Stay strong my niece.

All my love,

Sheryl K. Toombs

My gaze drifted over to the notebook labeled **Life 7: Human 4**. I had to admit I was curious. Sheryl always had a flair for the dramatic; I could only imagine what she had written and convinced herself held such weight. I reached into my bag for my flask and drank a healthy gulp. Whatever I had poured into it burned on the way down. A hiss pulled past my lips as I stared at the letter again. I couldn't make a decision today. I had to prepare for my mother's arrival. After a few minutes and finishing the contents of the flask I showered and got ready to pick up my mother from the train station.

An hour later I sat in the train station waiting for the telltale rumble of the rafters above my head that announced the train's arrival. I had come out to Coverton a few days before my mother to prepare everything. When we had gotten the call about my aunt, my mother had handed over the phone immediately, refusing to talk to anyone about it further. To be honest I didn't see why she was even coming to the service. The rafters rumbled, knocking down a faint sprinkle of sawdust on my head. I brushed away the debris from my jacket and walked closer to the arrivals door. A few moments later, I recognized the slick black hair of my mother as she came around the corner. She was carrying a small bag which was evidence that she did not plan on staying any longer than the night. My aunt's memorial service was scheduled for the afternoon, and my mother's ticket was already purchased for the train ticket back to Atlanta tomorrow morning.

"Come get these bags, girl," she snapped shoving the bag into my arms.

"Glad you had a nice trip mother," I huffed as I lifted the bag onto my shoulder.

I plastered a smile onto my face. Honestly, I had not expected my mother to come. Every time I mentioned Sheryl's name in the past I was met with a curled lip and what only could be described as a look of pure disgust.

"How long until this service?"

"Two hours, mom."

A huff pulled past her lips, and she took a few steps ahead of me. Just as I opened my mouth to speak I fell forward as someone shoved me from behind. I turned to face my attacker coming eye to eye with a blonde woman who smelled of menthols and burned coffee. Her breath was coming out in sharp pants, and warm spit sprayed onto my cheek.

"Be warned child of Persephone," she spat.

A larger man rushed over and dragged her off of me. My mom reached down to help me to my feet and knocked the dirt from my shoulders.

"Who is Persephone?" my mom stared after the woman still trying to break free from the man's grasp.

"I don't know mom. Let's just go."

I turned on my heel and rushed out the door.

Two hours later I flattened my shirt and tucked it into my dress pants. The dark blue button-up popped out again as I reached to grab my blazer off the chair next to the mirror. Sitting in the chair was the notebook and note my aunt had left. I tucked the notebook into my bag and shrugged the strap onto my shoulder.

"The car is here," my mom yelled from the window.

When we went downstairs, a small black compact car from the funeral home was idling on the sidewalk. I could feel the eyes of the townsfolk watching us as we stepped into the car and pulled away.

Coverton Memorial boasted no frills or even flowers. The people buried there were the forgotten citizens. They were outcasts whose families only remembered them when the coroner matched their fingerprints or dental records. My aunt would be buried here amongst the forgotten, but she would be the only one with a headstone marking her final resting place. Sporadic clumps of flowers and weeds spouted from the other graves. The life leaching plants were the only evidence that a body was buried. I stepped out onto the small gravel road and picked my way around the clumps of flowers until I reached the freshly opened hole in the ground that waited to swallow the mahogany box that held the shell my aunt once occupied.

"We are gathered here today to honor the life of Sheryl Toombs," the priest began placing a gentle hand on top of the closed coffin.

"How long is this going to take?" my mom huffed adjusting the black sunglasses on her face and pretending to wipe tears from her eyes.

"I told him to keep it short," I replied, clenching my jaw.

From the corner of my eye, I saw movement among the trees. I turned my head slowly to look into the mass of thick trees and vines that grew around the cemetery, encasing the death in the clearing and shielding it from the rest of the town. There was nothing there. As I turned back, I couldn't shake the feeling that someone was watching me. The same cold tingle crawled up my back and settled in my neck making the hairs stand on end. I turned around fully this time my eyes meeting golden orbs staring at me from the trees. There were four people gathered at the edge of the cemetery each of them cloaked in long black billowing robes that caught the wind and whipped leaves into a frenzy around them. I tugged at my mother's sleeve begging her to look but refusing to turn around and lose the sight of the apparition. Behind me the priest droned on, and I could hear the clatter of dirt against the wooden coffin. A forceful wind blew up from the trees kicking up dust and forcing me to shield my eyes.

"What was that?" my mother spat out dirt and knocked the speckled flakes from her jacket.

My eyes shot back up to the line of trees, but the only thing mixed among their branches were clumps of kudzu wrapped around old tires and bits of trash that had found their way into the clearing. The click of the crank starting up and lowering the casket broke me out of my thoughts just as another shiver flew down my spine. I grabbed my mother by the shoulder and dragged her back towards the car. A voice in my head told me to run, to get out of the clearing, to get as far away from the cemetery as possible. I jerked open the car door and pushed my mother down into the seat.

"What's gotten into you, child?" she spat shoving my hand away from her shoulder.

"Mom, stop talking for a minute." My ears prickled as a strange sound drifted across the grass towards me.

Was someone singing?

"I don't know who you think you're talking to…"

"Sir, can we go?" I asked the driver the funeral home had sent.

He was standing at the edge of the trees smoking a cigarette. The smoke billowed up and around his face as a sickly grin spread over his lips. He dropped the cigarette into the grass at the edge of the property and began walking towards me. The singing got louder. The voice was back in my head, telling me to get in the driver's seat and drive. Get out of there. Run! But I was frozen in place as a mass of people in black robes slid through the trees towards me.

"Etiam mors necesse mori," the man chanted as he stepped closer.

I slammed the door shut on my mother and bolted around the car and slipped into the driver's seat.

"Etiam mors necesse mori," the voices of the robed figures reverberated in my head.

I clutched at the steering wheel, trying to focus. My knuckles turned white on the wheel as I raised my eyes to the rearview mirror. My mother was watching the figures coming towards us. Her mouth was agape and twitching like she was attempting to say something.

“Etiam mors necesse mori,” the voices boomed again.

I could see them coming towards me, but their voices bounced in my head sending a shock of blinding white heat racing through my skull. I reached blindly for the keys, but my hand reached only the cool metal of the ignition.

“Etiam mors necesse mori,” the voices were quieter this time.

I sat up gasping for breath as I saw the figures retreating into the woods again. The pain in my head eased to a dull ache as I watched one of the figures turn and nod towards the car. I reached into the backseat for my bag. Just as my fingers met the rough fabric, my mother’s fingers slipped over mine. A tremble passed through my body as I looked up into her eyes. She stared past me, and a smile slowly spread across her face.

“Etiam mors necesse mori,” she whispered and brushed a strand of hair from my cheek.

Her fingers were cold.

“What does that even mean?” I asked my voice cracked despite my effort to keep it controlled.

“Even death must die,” she purred.

Then the world went black.

4

Darkness.

I blinked a few times trying to ensure myself that my eyes were open before I leaned forward to press two fingers to my burning temple. Stickiness coated my fingertips, and I assumed I must be bleeding. The soft cacophony of chirping crickets and the crackle of tree limbs breaking in the distance surrounded me. My head lifted to look around. I was still in the car from earlier.

"Mom," I gasped my gaze shooting behind me to the backseat that now sat empty.

My bag was still on the seat. I pulled it into my lap and tentatively opened the flap. The notebook was still there accompanied by the smell of burned paper. Had someone tried to burn the pages? Pushing the notebook back down into the bag, I reached for the ignition remembering that the driver had the keys. I squinted trying to make out any silhouettes outside the window, but only darkness stared back. A chill raced down my spine as I slowly opened the door and stepped outside. The coarse gravel of the makeshift road crunched underneath my feet as I walked forward past the car, my bag clutched firmly in my hands as I walked out of the cemetery. My eyes frantically scanned for any signs of life or light to help me find my way out of the grove of trees. The gravel path suddenly stopped, and I tentatively stuck out a foot, testing the ground in front of me that I couldn't see. As I pressed my foot down, the ground gave way slightly, and I slipped crashing in a pile, the gravel stabbing into my back. I eased myself back up to my feet, wincing as I felt a new sting growing in my side; the headache still throbbed behind my eyes. This time as I stepped off the path I steadied myself on what I could only assume was mud and began walking up what I guessed was a dirt road.

The faint chirping of crickets no longer met my ears, and there was only silence and the squelch of my shoes in the dirt.

Suddenly, I heard another sound. I stopped, my ears straining to hear in the darkness, my eyes searching for the source of the sound. A tiny light began to flicker yards away, slowly making its way towards me through the trees. It wasn't the eyes from earlier, but I still stumbled until I found the shallow ditch that I knew lined the dirt road. The light came closer, weaving back and forth through the trees. As it drew closer, I heard another noise. A name whispered frantically in the darkness.

"Ky! Ky!" the voice hissed.

I pressed my back to the cold mud of the bank and looked over, keeping my head obscured as much as I could. The figure was a man dressed in all black. I didn't recognize him until the light glinted in his bright blue eyes.

"Trent," I whispered, standing up fully.

The light found me seconds later, and he slipped down into the bank next to me, pulling me into a hug.

"Oh my god, Ky. I'm so glad you're okay," he said, shining the light in my eyes, "Are you hurt?"

"Not too bad. There's a cut on my head, and I'm pretty sure I bruised my hip. What are you doing out here?" I asked, my voice echoing through the trees.

"Remember I told you we were investigating that cult. We got a tip about some strange activity at the cemetery."

"What took you so long?"

"You can't go rushing in unprepared."

"How long does it take you to prepare a flashlight?"

Trent laughed then helped me up to the bank. A bright light washed over us as other black-clad figures emerged from various spots in the trees. Trent nodded to them and wrapped an arm around me. The headlights of a car slowly made its way towards us; he ushered me into the backseat and hopped in the front. I recognized the driver as Agent Cortell, and with a nod, she slowly pulled off down the road. With a sigh, I pressed my head to the cold pane of the window watching as the agents swept through the forest. As one of them moved closer to the road, I noticed for the first time that the mud I was stepping in earlier wasn't mud. It was red clay. I sat up a little straighter and squinted; the color of the clay seemed a bit off. As the light swept over the area again, my breath caught in my throat. It wasn't clay at all. It was blood-soaked dirt and amongst the trees where I had just come from lay bodies, the headlights of the car illuminating them for the first time as we drove past.

"Trent…my mother…she," I stammered as I looked down at the dirt clinging to me.

"She's fine. She's at the hospital. Thinks you were in a car accident," he answered.

I nodded, but my eyes never left the delicate crust of red slowly drying on my clothes and shoes. I could feel clumps of it sticking in my hair. My hand reached up to pull a clump lose, wrapping around something hard. When I pulled away, I had to squint now that we were further away from the agents and their flashlights. I reached up and flicked on the car light immediately regretting the decision as my eyes settled on the bone shard in my hand.

"T…T…Trent," I stammered the bone was lying bloody on my palm as I held it out to him.

He turned around to look at me; his eyes went wide for a second before he pulled out an evidence bag from the dash and zipped the bone in it. Once the bone was gone, he replaced it with his hand.

"Hey, you're safe now. Just relax." He let go of my hand and turned back towards the front.

I leaned back into the seats, my head thudding against the headrest. A shaky breath pulled past my lips.

"She's remarkably calm about this whole thing," Agent Cortell whispered.

Trent smirked and chuckled under his breath, his eyes darting back over the seat towards me. I breathed in and out again, closing my eyes and trying to control the tremors I could feel building low in my body. The tremors got stronger, thrumming their way through my fingers and down my arm. They grew worse, the trembles fluttered through my chest and made it hard to breathe. Gray spots danced in my vision, the calming breaths I was trying to take failing. My fingers gripped into the material of my shirt, the ooze of dried blood and dirt leaking between my fingers made my breath hitch again. The gray spots danced again, increasing in number, darkness fading in along the edges.

"Trent," I gasped, leaning forward, my fingers scrambling against the seat next to his shoulder.

"Ky," his eyes met mine across the seat just as I faded into unconsciousness again.

5

The smell of bleach and disinfectant was the first thing to assault my senses, before the lights overhead and rapid beeping of the heart monitor next to my head. A streak of blue flooded into my vision as a nurse arrived to turn off the monitor. Seconds later, I felt the cool press of her fingers against my shoulder before my eyes flickered up to hers. A blinding light from the pen in her hand replaced her deep green eyes. She nodded once before slipping back out the door and down the hall. Seconds later Trent slid into the room with a vase full of chrysanthemums. I winced, eased myself up straighter and sighed into the pillow as my body settled into the new position. I felt the bed dip for a moment as he sat down, but I refused to meet his eyes. I wanted to forget the truth if only for one moment more.

"Ky," he spoke, softly running his fingers along the back of my hand.

Outside the window of the hospital, I could see the rooftops of Atlanta apartments. The one closest to the hospital bore a rooftop pool where tenants lounged around the edges. A few of them splashed each other in the pool carefree and oblivious of the horrors racing through the mind of the woman staring at them. My room was far up enough that the usually deafening sound of cars and people bustling about the city became a steady drone in the background. The noise blended in with the beep of machines in other rooms and the swish of scrubs as nurses and doctors hustled around to do their rounds.

"Ky," he repeated, forcefully this time.

I slowly turned my head towards him; an invisible hand seemed to squeeze at my throat when I saw the sadness in his eyes.

“My mom…is she,” I stammered, blinking back the tears threatening to spill down my cheeks.

“She’s fine. I told you that…you were the only two that survived the massacre.”

“Massacre? Did someone plan that? What kind of person kills people at a funeral? Then the people in the woods and the singing,” my words poured out of my mouth before my brain could even decide what I wanted to say.

“Ky. Breathe.” He placed a comforting hand on my shoulder, waiting until my breath slowed.

From his pocket, he pulled a thin sheet of paper; sketched onto the page was the symbol of a deer with a wreath of flowers around its head. My heart fluttered for a moment. That symbol seemed familiar to me, yet I couldn’t recall where I had seen it before.

“Have you ever heard of a group called the Children of Persephone?”

"No," I frowned before gasping, "wait…that's what the lady at the train station called me."

"Really?" Trent shifted on the bed, his eyes becoming darker with concentration.

"Yeah. I was strange. She knocked me over and said be warned child of Persephone."

"Can you describe this woman?"

"Blonde, older, kind of thin, obvious smoker. Why does this matter?"

"You could be in danger Ky. Did you aunt leave you anything?" Trent stood abruptly, rubbing his hands along the side of his pants.

It was a habit of his if he was nervous or excited, and right now, I couldn't tell the difference. He ran a hand over his head, wiping sweat from his brow as he turned towards me again.

"Ky, listen to me. This is crucial. Did your aunt leave you anything?"

"Technically no. She died with a notebook in her hand, and I have that."

Trent paused, his eyes boring into mine, and for the first time, I was frightened of him. He slowly made his way back up to my side, his eyes bright against the fluorescent lights of the hospital.

"Do you have it with you?"

"Yeah. It's in my bag," I said, pointing to the bag sitting on the small table next to my bedside.

Trent reached for the bag, but I stopped him, pulling it to my chest instead. He reached for it again, and I pushed him away despite the sting it sent through my hand as the IV shifted. After staring at me for a moment, he sighed and sat down on the edge of the bed again. This time his expression was calmer and more the Trent that I knew.

"I need to see that book, Ky," he said slowly, anger still dripped in his voice despite the calm demeanor he was trying to maintain.

"No."

"Dammit, Ky," he slammed his hand down on the table.

My heart monitor simultaneously went off as I jumped and clutched my bag tighter. His fist slammed into the wall as he mumbled a string of curses under his breath. The heavy thud of his footsteps seemed to echo around the room, entombing me with their sound as he paced back and forth muttering. My finger rapidly tapped for the call button. No one came. Could they not hear the monitor screaming as my heart thundered in my ear?

"Is everything okay?" a voice finally broke through the cacophony of sounds in the room.

“Yes. Everything is fine,” Trent smiled, leaning against the window sill.

He casually tucked his thumbs into his pockets and smiled at the nurse. She smirked and turned towards me; my expression was far less calm as I clutched the bag to my chest and pulled my knees in closer.

“I want to see my mom,” I whispered, wanting to be anywhere except in this room.

“I’m sorry, that isn’t possible, Ms. Toombs. Your mother was flown to LA thirty minutes ago where they could treat her better.”

“I thought you said she was okay?” I frowned, anger poured off my body in waves as I stared down Trent who still stood smirking against the window.

“She is, you want your mom to get the best care, right?”

"I…I guess so." I agreed, but I couldn't shake the eerie feeling sitting heavy on my chest.

I could still see the figures gliding through the trees, hear their voices in my head, feel the blood-stained mud under my fingers. I had to get out of here, but that voice was back telling me to be careful and bid my time.

Later that day, I was released from the hospital. I had spent the rest of the day asleep in a ball in the hospital bed with my backpack clutched to my chest. In the haze of sleep, I thought I saw a figure slowly approaching my bedside, their hand extending towards my chest. I had startled awake but saw no one and decided to stay awake the rest of the afternoon until I was released. As I sat on a bench outside the hospital waiting for a cab to take me to the rental car shop I tentatively opened the backpack again. The notebook was still safely tucked inside, the edges slightly singed but intact. I pulled the note from the notebook; my fingers traced over the careful swoops of Sheryl's writing.

The cab ride was uneventful; the driver steadily droned about how terrible it was to be a cab driver in the city. I rested my head against the window of the cab, my eyes flickering shut despite the ride to the rental agency only being a few minutes long.

After renting a car, I made my way from the rush of the city to the eerie calm of the countryside. The din of people and vehicles faded away as I approached Coverton once again. The sound vanished as I made my way back into the woods to Sheryl's house. Trees stood guard over the narrow dirt road that weaved its way through the middle of them. No lights lined the drive leading to her home. Further up the street, the last streetlight flickered ominously at the beginning of the dirt road. Even though the high beams of the car were on, it was nearly impossible to see more than a few feet ahead. The only thing that kept me moving forward was the shine of the moonlight off in the distance, marking the small patch of cleared land where her house loomed.

The night stood still around me as I pulled up to the rusted metal gate marking the final portion of the drive to the small wooden home tucked into the woods. I stepped from the car, my eyes darting along the treeline. The feeling of being watched crept up my neck again. I tried to shake it off and chalk it up to my paranoia. The same paranoia that liked to play games with me and sent me racing to my car late at night, convinced that a serial killer or robber lurked nearby ready to strike at every darkened corner. Rust flaked away on my fingers as I pushed the gate open and climbed back inside the car, wiping my hands along my jacket. The stain stood dark against the fabric like blood…my mind flashed back to the cemetery. The ground. The bodies. The bones scattered across the field. A shudder raced down my spine as I refocused on the task at hand. I slowly made my way down the overgrown, muddy drive. The tires of the SUV I had rented sank into the ground and threatened to stick. I continued until I could see the house in the distance.

The house was awash with a sickly yellow glow from the lamps perched just outside the door. As I made my way up the steps, I hesitated for a moment. My ears searched for the skittering sound that I swore I heard moments before. I chanced a glance over my shoulder but saw nothing except the fading LED lights of the car and the looming forest around me. I reached for the handle of the door, and it opened without much effort. The sight that met my eye made me want to turn back, and I hesitated for a moment. That moment was all I needed to hear the skittering sound in the trees again and hear the voice in my head telling me to hurry.Someone had ransacked Sheryl's home. The furniture lay toppled over onto its side, cupboards emptied onto the floor, and chunks were missing from the walls exposing the wiring behind it. I slowly made my way through the wreckage of the home, carefully stepping over broken glass and shards of pottery until I reached the master bedroom. My mind traveled back to a faint memory of spending a holiday with my aunt. It was one of the few times the family got together aside from funerals and the occasional wedding. Sheryl always loved to play Jenga, and I was always fascinated by her ability to remove even the hardest block from the stack. The patchwork of wooden panels that line the walls of her bedroom were similar to the game. I ran my hand over slightly splintering wood, each board giving away slightly under my fingers. I could tell that someone had tried to rip them from the walls from the scratches that seemed to be made by a crowbar. Just to the left of her nightstand one panel seemed more solid than the rest. I pushed hard against the panel trying to get it to slide inward, but it didn't budge.

Careful touch reaps more reward than brute force.

I could hear Sheryl's voice saying the phrase as she carefully removed another block, leaving the tower of logs precariously formed but balanced none the less. I softly pressed against the side of the panel, and it slipped back into an indention in the wall behind it. Tucked into the small space was a brown leather satchel. Emblazoned on the front was a gold and crimson pomegranate. My fingers traced the slightly raised symbol, a tingle raced down my arm, before disappearing as quickly as it came. I shouldered the satchel and looked around the modest bedroom.

On the nightstand was a small collection of pictures. One was of Sheryl and my mother when they were younger, sporting pigtails and gap-toothed smiles. The others were of people I didn't recognize: a woman with hair like fire and a man with cold eyes standing outside a bookstore. Moonlight streamed through the bedroom window casting shadows across the floor like a bleeding pen in a pocket. Darkness flooded the window for a moment, and I froze, straining to hear anything that would tell me what caused the shadow that passed across the wall moments before. Then I heard it…footsteps so soft that if I weren't listening for something I would have assumed it was the patter of rodents across the hardwood. Slinking my way out of the bedroom and keeping the wall at my back I approached the front door. In a flash, I bolted outside and down the steps to my car. My hands dropped unceremoniously to my sides as I took in the destruction that lay before me. Tendrils of cloth billowed in the breeze from the slashed seats. The coffee I had been drinking on the way was upturned on the floor, and the tires all lay flat, slowly being swallowed by the indifferent mud. Fate did not allow me to feel anything but fear as a scream ripped through the night. The sound pierced the silence and sent my body into hyperdrive. Without another look around I began to run and kept running.

Mud caked around my ankles and feet, pulling me further and further into the mire with every step I took, but I kept running. A car door slammed behind me, another disgruntled groan, but I still ran until I reached the steady flickering streetlight at the end of the drive. Fire burned in my chest as I leaned against the light pole trying to catch my breath, but I only took a moment since I could hear the slow trudge of tires coming up the path behind me. I started down the road, keeping to the shadow of the trees; my ears strained past the sound of my heartbeat to listen for the tires, for any sound that I wasn't alone on the road. The faint squelching of tires was heard for a moment before the flicker of headlights wove its way down the path. My fingers twitched at the satchel on my side. The not even slightly heavy bag was the only semblance of a weapon I had. I slid the strap down my arm and looped it around my hand a few times, my fingers curling into the rough material as I continued walking. Chancing a glance over my shoulder, I saw the headlights become brighter as a car pulled around a bend and began to slow as it came closer to me.

"Ky?" a small voice called from the window as the car pulled up to me.

A short older woman, her black hair pushed back by a royal purple headband sat behind the wheel. She looked over her shoulder as another car's headlights lazily looped along the path in the direction from which she'd come. Her fingers white-knuckled on the wheel as she looked up at me, eyes wide and pleading. I nodded before slipping into the passenger seat, my fingers still tight in the strap of the bag as she drove off into the night. For a moment my mind chastised me, getting in a car with a woman I had never met, but the voice was there in my mind telling me to trust her.

After a few minutes, we were no longer on the dimly lit road and were making our way through the middle of the town. Just past the diner we turned onto a short road and pulled into a brightly lit home, soft white light flickered from sconces around the door. The light illuminated a partially closed in porch, a multitude of colorful doors enclosed the area, bright and inviting even in the darkness.

“Come in for some tea, and I’ll explain what I can,” the woman smiled before getting out of the car.

The thump of her hand pressed heavy against the hood of the car as she made her way up the short driveway. My eyes darted back to the cane sitting in the backseat, then to the woman shuffling into the home, clutching the doorframe along the way. I stepped out the car and made my way inside, closing the door behind me when I entered. The first thing I noticed was the paintings. Oil paintings covered every inch of the wall from floor to ceiling. Poised at the top of the stairs was the largest painting, a beautiful cityscape spread out across the canvas. My eyes recognized the towering skyscrapers of New York. Thin strokes of paint mimicked the chaos of cars and people on the streets below. I was drawn to the painting, my eyes noticing the small details that I hadn’t from the first floor. The swimmer in a rooftop pool. The reflection of spotlights from a theater in the distance. The couple swaying together in the window of an apartment building.

“I painted that when I was much younger. Before arthritis set in.” The woman leaned heavy against the bottom of the stairwell.

“It’s beautiful.” I smiled, making my way down the stairs and following her into the kitchen.

Steam drifted up from the cup of tea, the calming smell of Chamomile and honey wreathed around me and settled the skittish feeling I had since hearing the footsteps outside of Sheryl’s house. The woman stared down at her cup for a moment, before sliding a faded photograph across the table. I picked up the photo, a laugh bubbling past my lips at the image of my mother sporting a massive afro and yellow-striped flair legged pants. I recognized my aunt Sheryl next to her; her locs were much shorter then. The tightly coiled twists barely reached her shoulder.

"My name is Ola Gene Reynolds. I probably should have led with that back on the road, but I had to get you out of there," the woman sighed, sipping her tea.

"Probably, but I'm the one that got in the car anyway."

"True." We both laughed.

Ola put down her cup and stared up into my eyes as she spoke, "I grew up with your mother and aunt. We were thicker than thieves since we were little. I met Liza, your mother first. She was always up to something, convincing us to sneak into bars and covering for me when I stayed out late with Otis. Oh, Otis was worth getting in trouble for that's for sure. That man could—"

"Go back. My mother was a troublemaker?" I frowned.

"Yes child, but that's not the point. Your mother and I were best friends until I met your aunt, Sheryl. Those two were always at odds about everything. I swear they got to arguin' over something every other day."

"Do you know why?"

"Sheryl always had something that Liza wanted; I'm not entirely sure what. They would fuss for hours about how selfish Sheryl was for keeping whatever it was to herself. Your mother never forgave her, and as the years went by, they grew further and further apart. You know that part, right."

I stared down at the picture. The women in it looked happier, and if I were honest, it had been some time since I saw my mother laughing or smiling. It was hard to believe that the woman in the photo full of life and laughter was the same cold woman that I now knew. I had always given my mother a pass; after all, she was forced to grow up earlier after her parents died when she was young. She had met my father young, and he had quickly become her life. I could still remember the nights hearing them talk about moving away to a different state, the dreams that both of them had. I swallowed past the lump in my throat remembering the day I came home from school, bounding into the kitchen for a snack to find my father on the kitchen floor. His eyes were wide and focused on nothing. The phone clutched in his hand. The sound of the dial-tone buzzing loud in the silence until my mother's scream ripped through the room. The ambulance, lights flashing and sirens wailing even though he was gone. In hindsight, I think they did it for me. To give my preteen anxiety some semblance of hope, but I had watched enough shows to know that my father was dead. My mother had been cold after that, her usually bright smile, faded into a mask of indifference. He was buried in a neighboring city, closer to his childhood home. Until I left for college, my mother grew angry with the town and its inhabitants as if my father's death was the town's fault. Her anger persisted to this day, infected and spreading.

"Are you okay?" Ola's hand pressed warm against my own, the wrinkles along her hand a stark contrast to my own.

Her eyes were warm, as her fingers grasped around my wrist and squeezing gently. For the first time, her eyes settled on the bag at my side, and she shuddered, pulling her hand away. My eyes drifted down to the bag, the gold and crimson pomegranate shimmering softly in the lights above us.

"What do you know about them?" I asked.

"Not much, just stories. Be careful with those books Ky. If those stories are true, you could be in great danger."

"What? They're just journals…right?"

"I don't know. I wish I did. If you want to know more look for Miriam Lockhart. She was Sheryl's girlfriend."

"Her girlfriend? Why wasn't she at the funeral?"

"I…I think I've said too much. I'm tired now. You should leave now," Ola stammered, pushing away from the table.

She stumbled away from the table, gripping along the walls until she reached the stairs. I set my tea down and left; the door clicking closed behind me. A breeze sent the leaves on the porch dancing and skipping across the ground. I made my way down the street, the streetlights illuminating my path as I made my way through the clumps of teenagers and drunks along the sidewalk. The hotel was only a few blocks over, and I quickly made my way there, the bag tight against my side.

Once I was locked away in the safety of my hotel room, I took the notebooks from my bag and set them out on the floor. I placed them in what I assumed to be the correct order.

Life 1: Animal 1

Life 2: Animal 2

Life 3: Human 1

Life 4: Animal 3

Life 5: Human 2

Life 6: Human 3

Finally, I placed the notebook I had retrieved from Sheryl's hands along with the rest.

Life 7: Human 4

For a moment I stared at the books, my eyes looking for what could be special about them. They were all plain composition notebooks, with no designs or special marking on the outside. I flipped to the first page of the book labeled: Life 1. In the center of the first page was the silhouette of a fly. In the second the silhouette of a spider. The third had a guitar. As I reached for the fourth one, my phone rang, startling me and making me drop the notebook. It clattered to the ground as I scrambled to grab my phone and make my voice return to normal.

"Hello," I said with more confidence than I felt.

"Is this Khylia Toombs?"

"Yes."

"My name is Megan; I represent Carter and Associates. I am calling to let you know the reading of your aunt's last will and testament is to take place tomorrow afternoon."

"Oh. Right. Thank you."

"Thank you. Bye, bye."

With a click, the woman hung up, and I ran my hand through the mess of my locs. For the first time that day I took a moment to breathe, exhaustion finally settling into my body. A yawn ripped past my throat, and I trudged over to the bed. I laid down, my gaze staring up at the smoke-stained ceiling. I couldn't help but think about the day, and for the first time, I let the tears fall. The fear fought for purchase in my brain, winning over the sadness for the moment. At least ten people had died in that cemetery, their bodies scattered amongst the already weeping ground, and no one seemed to notice or care. Everyone was so calm and unphased as if large scale murders were a daily occurrence. Were they or had I always been so caught up in my own life that I hadn't noticed? Is that why the cemetery was shielded from view? The thoughts raced through my mind, my heart speeding up with every spiral of my mind. I fell asleep but was soon jolted awake as I imagined a phantom figure slowly guiding their way across the room towards the books. My body moved on instinct shielding the books from the phantom. A scream ripped through the silent air. Was it from my own throat or the person who tried to tear the notebooks from under me? My dream dissipated quickly, the figure a forgotten component along with it.

6

Bruised-cherry red carpet filled my vision as my eyes flickered open, the sunlight streaming through the open window bringing me out of the fog of sleep. My body ached as I stretched out my arms, several thuds resounded around the room as the notebooks dropped from my grasp. I squinted in the sunlight, trying to remember how I had ended up on the floor. The dream of the phantom figure came back to me in a flash, my heartbeat immediately picking up as I noted the new singe marks on the edge of the notebooks. My alarm went off moments later, a groan leaving my lips at the sound. I stretched out on the carpet for a moment, my fingers tracing absentmindedly along the pomegranate along the satchel. Electricity tingled through my fingers for a moment as I touched the bag. Sunlight poured through the window, illuminating the marking in a soft glow. With a final huff I forced myself to get ready for the reading of the will and my flight home immediately after.

Carter and Associates was the only long-standing law firm in the county. Every other practice had gone under a long time ago from lack of work and failed cases. The Carters, especially Megan Carter, the youngest of the clan were all lawyers. It was a well-known fact that their family legacy stretched back for decades. Their great grandfather was rumored to have served as the defender for numerous mobsters in his heyday. Nowadays, the Carters kept their family business afloat by taking odd cases in the city while maintaining their presence in Coverton by representing residents in smaller civil matters. The offices of Carter and Associates looked like a recommissioned speakeasy with paneled walls and brown leather couches. The leather creaked as I sat down on the end of a loveseat, my palms leaving wet streaks along the armrest. I was attempting to wipe it away when a tall black woman entered, her raven-black hair pulled up into a ponytail. Her eyes darted around the room, like a deer caught in the headlights before they finally settled on me. A smile slowly spread across her lips, her shoulders relaxing as she crossed the room. As she walked the royal purple dress she was wearing flowed behind her, my mouth going dry as she approached.

"You must be Ky," she smiled, extending a slender hand towards mine, a golden bracelet dangled from her wrist with a pomegranate made of rubies hanging from a small loop.

"Yes. You must be Miriam," I stammered, awkwardly scrubbing my hand across my jeans and shaking her hand.

"How did you know?"

"Call it a lucky guess. You were my aunt's gi…"

"Miriam Lockhart, it has been too long," a deep baritone voice boomed against the paneled walls.

Both of us turned to the voice; a large stocky man was making his way over to us. Steel gray eyes were a perfect complement to the man's short cut gray hair and beard. His eyes were piercing, but there was clear exhaustion in the lines of his pale face. Despite the tired gait in his walk he smiled and shook my hand then Miriam's.

"Arthur St. John, I would say it has been too long, but that would imply I take pleasure in your company," Miriam spat.

Before we could talk anymore, Megan Carter stepped from an adjoining room and ushered us all inside. Her eyes met mine, recognition fluttering there for a moment. I fixed my features and smiled politely, refusing to focus on the memories of high school Megan Carter who had started rumors about me because I used an unflattering picture of her in the school paper. We all sat down around the room while Megan pulled a thin envelope from an open box on a desk near her chair.

"Hello. We all know we are gathered here to read the will of Sheryl K. Toombs. Any questions?" Megan smiled.

No one spoke, but we all looked around at each other, an unease settled in my stomach. I shifted in my chair, making the leather groan again. Miriam reached over and patted my arm gently before nodding to Megan to continue.

"First I would like to say that this is a little unorthodox for us, since reading of the wills are an outdated practice, but Ms. Toombs requested it in her final wishes," Megan snapped open envelope, "I Sheryl

Kennedy Toombs being of sound mind and body, not acting under duress, upon my death declare the following for my estate."

Arthur and Miriam exchanged steely glances from across the room. Miriam's fingers played with the charm on her bracelet while Arthur's fingers drummed against the arm of his chair.

"To Miriam Lockhart, the love of my life, I give my art collection. Our love for oil on canvas brought us together, and I hope that every time you gaze upon a painting you will think of the fond memories we had together," Megan read.

Miriam sighed, a smile playing on her lips as she lowered her head. A stray tear raced down her cheek, but she quickly wiped it away, her expression settling into a mask of calm once more.

"To Khylia Toombs, my niece and only blood relative who doesn't consider me a loon, I leave all of my money and property," Megan smiled, "I'll get you the documents after the meeting."

I nodded in understanding and settled back into the chair, eyes focused on Arthur who was practically squirming in his seat. Megan read another short paragraph Sheryl included about her love for life, art, and her family before finishing. She frowned and looked over to Arthur her brow furrowed in confusion.

"I'm sorry Mr. St. John, there's nothing in the will for you. I guess my assistant made a mistake in contacting you," Megan apologized.

"It's okay, Mrs. Carter," Arthur smiled sweetly, "but I didn't hear a mention of a book collection. I know Sheryl was quite the collector of rare and unique novels."

"I'm afraid you're wrong, Arthur, Sheryl wasn't much of a reader," Miriam interjected.

"On the contrary, Ms. Lockhart. She was quite the bibliophile. Maybe you didn't know her as well as you claim."

"Why are you here, anyway? You two were far from friends."

"Touchy, touchy, touchy. Always so eager to fly off the handle," Arthur stood and strode over to Miriam, a smirk playing at the corners of his lips.

Miriam remained seated, but her eyes were dark with rage, hands clenching and unclenching into fists at her side.

"That's all for the day. Why don't we all just go our separate ways now? Khylia if you will stay for a moment please to receive the documents I mentioned earlier," Megan chimed in stepping between Arthur and Miriam.

"Of course, Mrs. Carter," Arthur lifted his hands in surrender and made his way towards the door.

Just outside the doorframe, he turned to look over his shoulder, the same sickly sweet smile on his lips.

"Be careful Miriam. Remember, sometimes keeping secrets is as dangerous as telling them," he sneered before leaving the room, the front door slammed in the distance behind him.

"I'm sorry about that Ky, Arthur and I have a bit of history," Miriam sighed, rolling her shoulders as if she were shrugging off the tension from a moment before.

"Yeah. I can see that. He said something about books?" I questioned, trying to gauge the look on her face, but it remained in the same stoic expression.

"Arthur says a lot of things. Enough about him. I would like to take you to lunch if you would like. I'm sure you have plenty of questions. I'll wait outside," Miriam smiled, leaving me alone with Megan.

Ten minutes later, I had sorted out what to do with my aunt's home and finances with a promise from Megan to stay in contact on the progress of my decisions. I stepped out into the muggy heat of a Georgia afternoon, coming up short when I saw Miriam waiting for me on the bench outside. One long stockinged leg jutted out from underneath the dress she wore as she scrolled through her phone. Even though she had offered to take me to lunch I hadn't expected the woman to stay. As if she sensed me, she looked up from her phone with a smile before joining me just outside the office door.

"I know most people hate The Dog Park, but I have to admit that Tommy makes a damn good shake," Miriam laughed as she walked away from me and down the sidewalk towards the diner on the corner.

I followed behind, doing my best to keep up with the older woman. Before we reached the diner, I could smell the burnt grease and overdone potatoes that tourists loved to indulge in at all hours of the day and night. Miriam smiled politely at everyone that passed by, some of them presses a tender hand to her shoulder and whispering their condolences. My presence only earned whispered words into ears when they thought were out of range.

Is that Ky?

Ms. Hotshot thinks she's too good for this town.

I heard she had her mom sent to a home.

She's always been stuck up.

A sudden gust of wind blew up around me; I tugged at the sleeves of my jacket, jogging to catch up with Miriam who was already entering the diner.

The diner was a new edition to the town along with the hotel. Growing up everything had closed at 10 pm, but then Tommy Garf, son of former mayor Jesse Garf had returned to Coverton. He was high on flunking out of Yale and looking for something to do with his daddy's money and decided to open the diner. It was a move that upset most of the senior members of Coverton, but they yielded when they realized that they would rather their kids be in a shady diner at 2 am than in a cow pasture or barn doing Lord knows what. The Dog Park or The Park as it was usually called, was your basic diner. They sold hotdogs, hamburgers, lukewarm cups of coffee and slices of cake made by the lead usher at the Baptist church. The Park's claim to fame, however, was a sandwich called the Toddzilla. Its name paid homage to one of Tommy's college friends: a five-pound burger topped with eight slices of cheddar and swiss, three fried eggs, nacho cheese, and a pound of onion rings or fries depending on your taste. No one ever ordered it except for tourists and locals that wanted to get E. Coli from the severely undercooked meat.

The first thing you notice about The Dog Park is the dogs. There were nostalgic paintings of dogs playing poker and the Maltese A Lisa. The entire restaurant was decorated in dog-themed décor, down to the Pug faced jukebox in the corner. Miriam sat down on the barstool made to look like an upturned fire hydrant, a long sigh hissing past her lips. I sat down next to her, eyes flickering to a picture behind the counter of Tommy and Jesse Garf at the groundbreaking for the diner. The picture had been printed in sepia to make it seem old. A single frame next to it boasted the first dollar the restaurant ever made. I couldn't contain the snort that escaped from my lips.

"It is a bit much," Miriam laughed, motioning for the waitress to come over.

"Welcome to The Dog Park, where you're sure to have a howling good time. What can I get you today?" the girl recited from memory; her face fixed in an uninterested smile that would fool tourists well enough.

"Kennel fries and two Doggone Good shakes," Miriam ordered smoothly.

The waitress wrote down the order then slid into the kitchen in the back. For the first time, I noticed the horrendous outfit she was wearing. The outfit was made to resemble a Dalmatian and was complete with a tail slowly swishing behind her as she walked away. We sat in silence as we waited for our food, the waitress returning moments later with a towering plate of fries and two shakes precariously balanced in her hand. Kennel fries were Tommy's version of poutine. A plate of crinkle cut fries were slathered with mushroom chili and bite-sized balls of deep-fried cheese.

Similarly, the Doggone Good shakes were a beast of Tommy's own invention. Chocolate and peanut butter ice cream blended with milk and chunks of dog treats which were just a mix of shortbread and pretzel cookies dipped in chocolate. The glass was the best part of the shake, sporting a massive straw to suck up the cookie pieces with a strip of bacon and a chicken wing flat pushed onto the straw. As I stared down the mountain of food, Miriam began to dig in, pulling a forkful of the fries and popping it into her mouth.

"Sheryl hated my love for fast food," she muttered through a mouthful of melted cheese.

I took a bite of the fries, pleasantly surprised that they were palatable considering the local teens that I know cooked the food. We diminished the fries to a small pile of mushrooms and a singular ball of cheese on the plate. It was only then that I turned to tackle the shake, waiting for Miriam to start talking.

"Your aunt and I met when we were in our 20s. We met at an art gallery where I was showing my work.

She had come to support her friend Ola. I believe you met her last night." Miriam played with a stray line of ice cream dripping down the side of her glass.

"How did you know I met?"

"Sheryl was special…she knew how to make everyone feel special and loved. I'm going to miss her," she sighed, playing with the charm on her bracelet.

"What does the pomegranate mean?"

"This marks me as a child of Persephone. Your aunt was a child, as well."

"Child of Persephone? What is that?"

"There are some things better left unsaid. I'm afraid I can't tell you."

"Is it about the notebooks she left?"

"Notebooks." Miriam's head whipped towards me, "what notebooks?"

"She died with a notebook in her hand and left me a letter telling me where to find the others."

"Did you? Find the others?"

Miriam's eyes were alight with joy as she waited for my answer. I refocused my attention on the shake for a moment before answering. There was no voice in my head this time, no sinking feeling as I opened my mouth to speak.

"Yes," I said, opening the satchel I had brought with me to show her the notebooks tucked safely inside.

"You have been given a great gift Ky. Guard this gift with your life."

"What if I don't want this supposed gift?"

"Then give them to someone that will protect them," Miriam fired back, her hand slamming onto the countertop.

"Why are they such a big deal? They're just journals."

"You have no idea the information you hold, give them to me." Miriam reached out attempting to take one of the notebooks from the satchel but jerked away just as quickly.

The edge of the notebook she had touched was smoking. I pulled the bag away and closed the satchel quickly. Miriam sighed, her eyes filling with tears as she cupped a hand over her face.

“I’m so sorry, Ky. I had no right. I should have known. Sheryl never made a mistake,” Miriam breathed out slowly, “If you accept Sheryl’s gift come find me and I will tell you everything you want to know.”

Without another word, Miriam threw a handful of cash on the counter and left in a flash of purple. My stomach churned, but I didn’t know if it was from the food or the anxious feeling thrumming through my veins. I turned to slide off the stool and crashed into a busboy carrying a tray of plates. Half-eaten fries and ketchup spilled all over the floor and my shirt. The boy scrambled to hand me paper towels to clean it up.

“It’s okay,” I tried to smile, the gesture faltering as my eyes focused on the ketchup spattered across the ground.

I was in the cemetery once more, the figures in hoods surrounding me before exploding in streaks of red across the ground. The shout asking if I were okay barely registered in my mind as I burst from the diner, gulping down breath after breath of muggy air. Faces turned my direction as they passed, but not a single person stopped to ask if I was okay. I focused instead on the sidewalk, the steady line of ants making their way through the cracks in the pavement, one in front of the other. As I focused on their constant track my breath began to even out, so I continued the same, listening for nature around me instead of the hum of people and the city oblivious to the horrors I had seen. After what felt like hours but was merely seconds, I straightened up and made my way back to the hotel to call a cab.

Twenty minutes later, I was on my way to Atlanta in what would have been the most expensive cab ride of my life had the police department not paid for it. They pitied me because of my aunt's recent passing and the "vandalism" that they called the destroyed rental car I had left behind. They attempted to convince me that I was the victim of criminals collecting parts for a chop shop, but I wasn't convinced they would get much for slashed tires or torn seat covers. Nevertheless I was grateful for the over $100 bill being footed by the CPD, and I was ready to leave the forsaken town behind. On the way to the airport I couldn't help but read the letter Sheryl had left for me once more. The curiosity of what these books held and why I seemed to be the only one able to touch them became too much.

7

After reaching my gate I slid down the wall in a corner and tentatively opened the notebook labeled Life 1: Animal 1. A nervous flutter raced through my veins, and for a moment I reconsidered reading. Maybe I should just give the notebooks to Miriam and leave whatever this was behind. I read through the ominous message in the letter I was given once more, took a deep breath and began to read.

Life 1: Animal 1

(Calliphoridae)

In my first life I was born into nothingness.

Life was strange and new. I knew I was born the 37th of 75 children to a mother that was only 12. Most people would think she was too young to have us, but if they knew that she was at death's door, maybe they would understand. Out of my numerous brothers and sisters I was only close to three of them, the others quickly faded into lost memories that I'm not entirely sure were real anymore. My mother did her best to keep us safe in the darkness, keeping us warm as we grew and learned. I was three when my mother died, leaving all of us formless and warm in the darkness still. I could feel myself growing and changing, the sensations of warmth and the presence of my siblings were no longer a comfort and instead felt crowded. Their presence was a suffocating weight that I couldn't escape even if I tried.

My awareness grew day by day as I burst forth and journeyed around the bright red, warm space. Later I would recognize the space as a dead animal. My presence being evidence of its decaying condition. A marker of death. I continued to grow and change, my hopes of freedom and adventure outside the bright red warm space grew as time passed. However, at seven my freedom was taken, and I found myself thrown into darkness once again. I knew I was still in the bright red warm space, but I could no longer see or move. My body was locked away inside of darkness while I grew and dreamed of freedom. It seemed like a year passed in the darkness and just as suddenly as I was locked away I came bursting forth once again into the light. My siblings were still there, but all of us were so different now. Fully formed, and almost the exact image of our mother long gone. A breeze ruffled past my body and the sensation alerted me to a new part of myself — thin little extensions of my body that caught the wind. I tested them once, twice, a third time before my brain registered what they were. Wings. These thin pieces gave me what I sought for so long— freedom from the bright red warm space. Even the space had changed; its once red welcoming and firm was brown and rotting away. I couldn't help but feel like it was my fault. With every step across the expanse, my feet sank heavy into its depths. I flitted my wings as I slowly lifted away from my siblings and out into the world around me that moved much slower than I did. A large animal with a black and gray arm lumbered towards me, but I effortlessly moved out of its way. Every speck of dust seemed to hover and shimmer suspended in the air as I flew by.

I found my home in a coop for animals that I would grow to know as chickens. Their wings were like mine but were thicker and clunky instead of thin and light. I loved someone when I was 15 and had children, but that part of my life seemed like a blur. I left the coop and settled in a can full of food where my children would never go hungry. My children left, and I began to grow tired. I decided to return to my home in the coop when I was twenty since all of my children were living on their own and the house with all the food was no longer full.

As I flew to my old beam that I loved, I felt something sticky touch my foot. I looked down to find a thin string wrapped around my foot and holding me fast. I flapped my wings hard, trying to free myself from the string but the more I struggled the tighter it seemed to coil. Another string stuck to my wing and as I struggled to free myself. I only got tangled more, an emotion I would come to know as fear began to build in my gut. Suddenly, I was spinning and a searing pain coursed through my abdomen. As darkness began to cloud my vision I looked up into eyes like mine, but larger. Another animal's bared fangs stared back at me. As the darkness took over once more I knew one thing. The darkness was always full of fear.

In my first life I was born a fly, and I learned that sometimes the price of freedom is fear.

I flipped through the remaining pages of the notebook. The rest of the pages were just a hodgepodge of pictures and diagrams of a fly's life cycle. Nonsense scribbles about the meaning of life and the name Persephone written over and over again filled the margins. I slipped the notebook back into my bag and leaned back against the wall behind me. I had hoped that the notebook would bring some sort of clarity to all of this, but it only confused me more. Was my aunt Sheryl studying insects or something? The din of the bustling airport around me returned, along with the smell of cinnamon, coffee, and cream cheese that made my mouth water. I watched as a young mother made her way over to the seat in front of me, her daughter happily munching on a cinnamon roll bigger than her tiny hand. The woman's face scrunched as she sat the little girl onto the faux leather seat. Both of them smiled at me for a moment; I could see the mom thinking hard as she stared at me. I sighed already knowing what she was going to say.

"Excuse me, could you watch her for a sec?" the woman smiled.

"Yeah, sure," I smiled back despite feeling awkward staring at the child swinging her feet back and forth in front of her.

The woman left, and I stood to sit next to the small girl in the empty chair. She immediately turned and reached her cream cheese icing covered fingers out to touch my hair. I gently moved her hand away and handed her one of the napkins in the bag.

"My name's Tiffany," the girl smiled up at me, a few teeth missing from the front of her mouth.

"I'm Ky," I smiled back.

"I like cinnamon rolls. Do you?"

"Yeah. They're pretty good."

"Want a bite of mine?"

“No. Thank you, though.”

“My mommy says it's nice to share.”

“Yeah. Have you ever been on a plane before?”

“No. Do you think your friend wants a piece?” the little girl frowned, looking over my shoulder.

“My friend?” I turned to look over my shoulder, noticing a younger woman staring at me from the other set of seats at the gate.

Our gazes met, and she quickly looked away. I turned back to the little girl who was still smiling. She took another huge mouthful of the slowly melting cinnamon roll in her hand still staring at me.

“That lady is looking at you again,” she said between mouthfuls.

I turned again, pretending to the look for the little girl’s mother but caught the woman’s eyes once more. At the same time, the girl’s mother came back carrying two iced coffees. She handed one to me as I stood and let her take my seat.

"Mommy, that lady over there was staring at Ky," the girl whispered to her mother.

I looked back in the direction the woman had come from, but the woman I had caught staring was nowhere to be seen.

Thirty minutes later, the boarding call for my plane resounded over the speakers, and I quickly made my way to the line. I was still searching for the woman from earlier, a tingle of fear crept down my spine. As I neared the front of the line, I saw her once more. Her eyes met mine before she turned away again, but not before I noticed the gold pin on her jacket.

"Excuse me miss, your boarding pass please," the TSA agent ordered.

"Yeah. Sorry," I stuttered, handing her my pass and making my way down the corridor.

The sounds of suitcase wheels and the steady whir of machinery seemed to entomb me as I made my way towards the plane. The little girl and her mother from earlier had boarded before me, the small child noticed me and waved happily as they stepped into the plane. I smiled back, chancing a glance over my shoulder to the sea of people making their way down the corridor with me.

Flying had always been a strange experience for me. Every flight I had ever taken was booked full, and I couldn't help but wonder why the people were going to the same destination as me. Were they on vacation? A romantic getaway? Work? Escaping from their everyday life to start over somewhere new? More than I would like to admit I would create stories for the people on the plane, trying to guess what brought their lives into such close proximity with mine. I wonder if other people did the same.

I stepped into the interior of the plane, smiled at the flight attendants as I passed and made my way to my seat. I looked down once more at my ticket, grateful for getting the window seat instead of the dreaded middle or aisle. The window seat was my favorite. It let me see the world unfolding underneath me like a cloth pulled away from a painting. More passengers spilled onto the plane, the sound of suitcases and duffel bags shoved into compartments and tucked way under seats filled the space around me. My eyes began to feel heavy, the exhaustion from the past few days settled on my shoulders, pulling me down into sleep. The rustle of someone sitting in the seat next to me startled me awake with a jolt.

"I'm sorry, I didn't mean to startle you," a soft voice said from the seat, a hand patting the back of my hand gently.

"It's o…" the words died on my lips as I came face to face with the woman who had been staring at me in the airport.

She was wearing a simple blue floral top and jeans with her hair tied up in a messy bun of dark brown hair, a pleasant smile on her face. Now that she was sitting next to me, I no longer felt the anxiety or fear from her stares earlier.

"It's alright," I responded finally, leaning over once again allowing the hum and pulse of the airplane engine to pull me into sleep.

Thunder crackled across the deep gray sky; the storm rolled fast across the landscape, flashes of lightning leading the way. My head tilted up towards the sky, watching the lightning dance across the sky like ballerinas on a darkened stage. The tendrils flickered in my eyes as I stepped off the porch. The wind whipped around me sending the remnants of the hay I had been bailing earlier across the yard. The rain beat down around me, washing everything anew and rusting the uncovered metal. As I walked, my boots sank into the mud as I made my way closer to the tree at the center of my property. A bolt of lightning streaked across the sky and struck the tree straight down its center, setting it ablaze for only a moment before being squelched by the rain. I made my way closer to the tree; my eyes fixed on the smoldering wood a few feet away.

"Ray?" A voice cries out behind me.

I turn towards the sound, but my vision is alight with a sudden flash of light. A searing jolt of red-hot pain pulses through my veins, my head is turning involuntarily upward towards the sky.

"Ray!" the same voice from earlier screamed.

8

I jolted awake; my head slammed back against the headrest of the airplane seat. The cabin was abuzz with chatter and flight attendants hastily walking back and forth. I scrubbed the trails of sleep from my eyes and with it the vestiges of the dream that I had been having for months now.

"What's happening?" I asked the woman sitting next to me.

"Emergency landing, they asked everyone to buckle their seatbelts," she explained.

"Right. Okay." I tugged at the seatbelt around my waist, my body trembling as if the electricity from the dream was still pulsing through my body.

"Are you alright?" the woman asked, gently placing a hand over the top of my trembling hand.

"I'll be okay. Weird dream."

A few seconds later the captain announced our descent into the airport. The ground below spread out in perfect little squares and miles of fields that seemed to go on forever. Arizona had a similar pattern, but there wasn't nearly enough desert to be that state.

"As we begin our descent into Cleveland, we ask that everyone remain buckled in. We apologize for those with connecting flights and will accommodate changes at the kiosk upon your arrival," one of the flight attendants chimed over the PA system.

I stared out the window as the plane slowly descended towards the tarmac. I could see a faint tendril of gray smoke spilling from somewhere near the wing of the aircraft. The chill of the air outside settled onto the window sending a shiver down my spine. I pulled the light jacket out of my bag and wrapped it around my shoulders, the notebooks showing for just a moment inside. When I looked up the woman was staring down into the bag. I hastily closed the flap and secured the bag between my feet.

After the plane landed, I made my way to the kiosk quickly, trying to beat the rest of the people filing off of the plane. The bite of the cold outside found me even inside of the airport, and I tugged my jacket around me tighter. As I approached the counter, the woman let out an exasperated sigh. The woman at the other counter next to me was bright red in the face and yelling at the exasperated ticketing agent.

"Hi, I need to get on the next possible flight back to LA," I smiled at the agent, trying to calm her fears.

"Of course. We don't have any flights to LA until tomorrow night, but Toledo has a flight out tomorrow morning," the woman stammered as if she was waiting for me to begin yelling.

"Is there someone who can call a cab for me?"

"Yes, miss," the woman breathed out, her shoulders relaxing immediately.

I fidgeted from foot to foot and waited for the woman to call a cab for me. My eyes wandered around the airport, settling first on the line behind me of people waiting to get new flights. The woman who had been sitting next to me on the plane was a few people behind me staring in my direction, but past me to the ticketing agent.

"Your cab will be here shortly. Cab pickup is down the hall and to the right. Keep walking straight until you get to the street. Cab number 657," the woman smiled, giving me my new ticket for the flight in Toledo.

"Thanks," I smiled.

I could feel the woman's eyes on me even as I walked away. I quickly made my way around the corner and out to the street. The airport wasn't nearly as big as the airport in Atlanta but was busy none the less. People weaved in and out of lines preparing to board their flights. A small kiosk was set up with sandwiches and chips just inside the doors. The small sign in front of the kiosk boasted that they were 100% airplane approved, whatever that meant. A small family of four were struggling to carry a massive cardboard box through the bag check. The father was barely holding onto the large awkward box, the mother shouting directions to "be careful," and reminding him he "better not drop the girls' things". I wondered what things the maybe four-year-old girls could possibly have that needed such a large box. I turned back towards the street and reached for the handle of the door when a loud metallic crash resounded behind me. Golden heads rolled around the floor as the father from earlier scrambled to pick up the pieces of the trophies that now lay scattered across the tile floor.

"Dammit Todd, they just won those," the woman earlier shouted.

"I know Cassandra," he fired back picking up the last of the trophies and slamming them into the box.

"Daddy, you broke our trophies," the taller of the two girls whined, her lip pouted out.

"Daddy is sorry," Cassandra petted, "aren't you daddy."

"Yes. I'm so sorry for dropping the box of participation trophies you won this weekend," he said through gritted teeth.

I turned to help him but stopped short when the woman from earlier came around the corner, our eyes locking across the room. I shoved open the door, leaving the man still scrambling and being yelled at by his wife. As I exited, the wind ripped through my coat, my teeth immediately starting to chatter. Seconds later, a muted orange cab pulled up to the curb; a bright-eyed blonde-haired woman popped out for a moment smiling.

"Are you Ky," the woman chirped, swiping hair from her eyes.

"Yeah," I said, glancing down to check the cab number.

"Mind if we split a ride," the voice of the woman from earlier said from behind me.

When I turned, she was standing impossibly close, a smile on her face, but she seemed to stare past me to the cab driver as she talked.

"I don't think so," I refused as politely as I could before opening the door and sinking into the stain crusted seat of the cab.

"I'll call my buddy for you," the cab driver offered before getting back in and pulling away from the curb.

As the cab pulled away from the airport, I chanced a look backward to see the woman still staring after the cab. The rush of the city faded into the zoom of a turnpike within minutes. I rested my head against the back of the seat, sighed, closed my eyes, and focused on the hum of the cab making its way down the turnpike. As my eyes fluttered closed, I noticed the glint of gold against the cab driver's shirt in the mirror. The small lantern pin was the last thing I saw before sleep claimed me again. My eyes flickered open sometime later, and we were still on the highway. I stretched, twisting to crack my back and noticed the dark green Beetle following behind us. The cab driver exited the freeway, slipping seamlessly into the countryside that opened up into wide flat land. Fields stretched out for miles around me in an endless sea of greenery, dotted with spots of brown from crops stripped down for the winter. I stretched again, my body revolting with crackles at the lack of movement for the past hour. Silently behind us on the roadway was the same dark green Beetle weaving its way down the road. If the road had been busier, the car would have been less visible, but the two cars were the only ones on the road.

"That's the same car," I said, slinking down into the seat.

"There are only a few airports with flights to LA, it's probably just another passenger headed to Toledo. Don't worry," the cab driver smiled, adjusting her mirror.

I nodded, despite the trembling I could feel building in my limbs and the rapid pounding of my heartbeat against its skeleton cage. A shock of green in my peripheral caught my attention. I turned to see a small island of trees amidst the rows of fields. From a distance the trees looked like an impenetrable fortress somehow untouched by the cultivation of farmland around it. Even from the road I could tell that the branches clung together like the ties of lovers thrust apart by fate. With a rumble of rocks under tires the cab turned on a pebble-strewn dirt road, the fortress of foliage looming in front of us as we continued down the path.

"Is this the fastest way to the airport?" I asked, hugging my jacket tighter around me as the chill from the outside set into my skin.

Momentary regret flickered into my mind at forgoing the heavyweight jacket in the airport lounge. My friends from the North always told me about the bitter cold, but I couldn't bring myself to buy the red and white striped Ohio jacket. It invited too many peppermint stick jokes into my mind. The thought dissipated as the once distant island of trees loomed ahead of us. Their once lush and wonder-filled branches seen from a distance quickly turned into a gnarled mess of branches like fingers reaching down towards the road. Seconds after entering the aisle of trees the main road vanished leaving only the path ahead of us and the never-ending forest of trees. Rocks crunched under the tires of the car, and I focused on following the thin sliver of light that I could see coming up between the trees. Bursting from the cove of trees a school bus sat covered in dead leaves and vines as the world slowly reclaimed it.

"Why is there a school bus out here?" I asked, taking out my phone and snapping a quick picture of the faded yellow bus.

"Some legends are best left unshared," the woman said softly, slowing the car until it stopped just beyond the clearing.

A tingling sensation shot up my spine, coupled with the urge to run again. I froze as the cab driver turned off the engine and stretched her arms.

"What are y…" I stopped short as my eyes met the cab driver's in the rearview.

"Etiam mors necesse mori," she smiled, her eyes slowly changing to the same gold color as the people from the cemetery.

My fingers scrambled for the door handle. It clicked uselessly from the child locks that had been turned on.

"Etiam mors necesse mori!" the woman shrieked as she launched over the middle console and into the backseat towards me.

Her hands went to my throat as my knee came up crashing into her stomach. The blow didn't phase her, and she continued to rip and claw at my face and hands. I fought back, my fists flailing uselessly as I tried to push her off me. As quickly as the attack started, it stopped momentarily as her eyes fixated on my bag, the edge of one of the notebooks was showing from being jostled around. I took her distraction as my chance and threw my weight against her, shoving her back towards the front seat where her head met the dashboard with a sickening crack. In seconds I had the child lock off and bolted from the car and down the road. Gravel slid under my feet causing me to stumble as I ran, the bag clutched to my side. The small voice in my head was there again, telling me to run until help arrived. Without warning an ear-splitting scream resounded from behind me, bouncing and echoing through the trees. My knees hit the ground hard, my hands coming up to grasp desperately at my ears as the same blinding white light from before pulsed in my vision. A hand grasped the back of my head, slamming my face down into the gravel. The warm slippery feel of blood dripped on the back of my neck as I struggled to throw my assailant off.

"Get off her," a calm voice said.

Seconds later, the weight was gone from my back, and I turned onto my back. The cab driver from earlier was struggling in the grasp of the woman from the airport. Blood gushed from a cut on the cab driver's head as she tried to break the sleeper hold she was trapped in. Dirt and gravel kicked up around us as the woman's legs struck out trying to find leverage. Her kicks slowed down as she faded into unconsciousness. With a smile the woman from the airport dragged the body back to the cab and returned to me moments later, extending her hand. I scooted backward on my hands, the voice was no longer there telling me to run, but I didn't fully trust the woman. How had she found me?

"It's okay, Ky," the woman smiled, reaching down to take my shuddering hand in her own.

As I rose to my feet, she dusted me off and pointed back to the green Beetle I had seen following the cab earlier. It was parked on the side of the road, blending in with the dense growth there.

"I called the cops. They're on their way." I said, my voice sounding a lot steadier than I felt.

"My name is Victoria. I was a friend of your aunt's," she said simply, slowly making her way into the trees toward the abandoned school bus.

"What? How did you know my aunt?" I stammered, following her and tucking the bag under my arm once more.

"This was my bus," Victoria sighed, trailing her fingers along the numbers on the front of the bus.

"What?"

"In my past life, my name was Edward. My wife and I had fallen on hard times, so I picked up a job as a bus driver. I hated those kids," she laughed, patting the bus again as she continued to walk around the side.

A trickle of something slipped down my neck, and I wiped at it frantically, my hand coming away bloody. It was then I remembered the cab driver bleeding on me earlier. When I looked up again, Victoria was holding out a handkerchief for me.

"Every day, I drove them to and from their gifted program. I listened to them talk about their dreams of being engineers, doctors, physicists. They were in elementary school, but I hated them just the same. I hated them for having dreams. I had dreams too once, but things didn't work out that way for me," Victoria pressed against the folding door of the bus, the material easily sliding back.

At the bottom of the steps, I noticed a dark stain that led up to the inside of the bus. Victoria sat down on the edge of the moss-covered seat and motioned for me to stand next to her. "I hated them for having hope. For being so carefree and optimistic not knowing that life could deal them a terrible hand like I had dealt me," Victoria huffed.

"What happened?" I asked, a sickening feeling began to build in my stomach.

"One day, we were on the way home. I was driving along that road right up there. I couldn't tell you how many times I had threatened them that I would drive off the road if they weren't quiet. I had said it so many times it had become a running joke…but that day. That day something was different. That day when I heard them talking about their futures and how bright they were, something snapped. I drove off the road, crashed through those trees right there," Victoria pointed to the gaping opening that the forest had left untouched, "I spun out, and the bus stopped right here. Before I passed out I could hear their screams, and after…there was just silence. I died later in the hospital. Every child on this bus died that day except for one little girl," Victoria wiped a stray tear from her cheek.

"Do you know what happened to her?" I asked, the sickening feeling tightened in my stomach like a boa constrictor.

"My mother told me a story when I was young about surviving a bus crash when she was nine. She would tell me that even though she could be angry with the man who did it, she wasn't. She said that anger is a virus that kills from the inside out. She taught me to hope, to believe that things could always get better and that true forgiveness is the greatest gift you can give to someone."

"Let me get this straight. You're saying you were the man that killed all your mother's friends when she was little…that you have lived another life before."

"Yes. I've lived six others. This is my last one."

An involuntary snort spilled from my lips as I stepped off the bus and walked back towards the main road. I could hear Victoria's footsteps behind me as I made my way down the dirt road as quickly as I could. My head throbbed from the nonsense story the woman had just told me, not to mention the knot I could feel forming where my head had met the ground. A soft hand grabbed my shoulder, pulling me up short.

"Ky, please. Let's talk somewhere else, and I'll try to explain the best I can," Victoria pleaded.

I stared down the endless dirt road in front of me, a chill settling into my skin as the sunlight began to fade in the distance. I was stuck in a place I didn't know, with a woman who could very well try to kill me too. My eyes met Victoria's pleading ones as she looked back towards the cab parked in the middle of the road.

"Okay," I nodded.

We quickly got into the car and drove the rest of the way down the road and out of the tangle of the trees. I closed my eyes, feeling my pulse thrumming in my chest. My breath shuddered into the cold air, making a small puff out in front of me. The dirt road led into a small sleepy town. Houses stood shoulder to shoulder with each other, their backyards blending into the next one. Soft orange light flickered against the back of one of the houses as people gathered around a bonfire. A truck was pulled up into the driveway, its lights shining bright to illuminate a group of teenage boys playing cornhole. Their laughter faded into nothingness as we continued through the town. A series of buildings stood guard over main street; their aging bricks reminded me of Coverton. One building, in particular, was covered in rusted doors and boarded windows except for the bright fluorescent-lit lobby of the post office. A few people milled about the streets, walking from the corner bakery that was closing down for the night. I watched as an elderly couple exited the building hand in hand, time-softened smiles on their faces as they turned off the lights and locked the door to their shop. After crossing a set of railroad tracks, Victoria pulled up outside of a small bar. The sign outside boasted, cold beer, pool and something called Charlie's chunks. Except for a set of trucks in the parking lot nearby, the street lay deserted. Victoria smiled softly and exited the car. The nervous energy from earlier was back, but it was nothing that couldn't be settled by a drink.

Upon entering the bar, the first thing I noticed was the signed pieces from racecars. Bumpers, car doors, and fenders all signed by their respective racers were bolted onto the walls. Checkered flags hung loosely around the bar, sandwiching in a menu of the daily specials. An older woman stepped out of the kitchen, a steaming plate of popcorn chicken and fries in her towel-covered hand.

"Be with you in a sec, Vicki," the woman smiled.

While we waited for the woman to return, I took the time to take in the rest of the bar. Three TVs were stationed around the bar that extended from just past the door to a back wall. Each one displayed the same baseball game and a rolling lottery game in the bottom corner. Despite the shabby appearance of the town, the bar was pristine. Every pool table boasted freshly brushed felt, polished balls and smooth pool sticks.

"What can I get you and your friend?" the elderly woman from earlier returned, her smile bright as she patted Vicki's hand.

"I'll take a beer," Victoria smiled.

"Same," I said, my eyes now transfixed on the set of pictures behind the bar.

The woman walked away from us before returning with two cold bottles of beer. She followed my eyes, smiling warmly as she looked at the pictures.

"That's my family. We've owned this bar for six generations. It's like a home to us. We treat her right, and she does the same for us," the woman explained before pointing to a particular picture.

"Who's that?" I asked, pointing to a dark-haired man that my eyes were suddenly drawn too.

"That's my brother Edward. He died a long time ago. He could have been a good man," the woman sighed, "let me know if you need something, Vicki."

Vicki watched the woman walk away, sadness showing in her eyes. I took a deep swallow of the beer, watching her closely.

"Did my story check out?" Victoria said, taking a sip of her beer.

"Huh?"

“I saw you googling my story. Did it check out?”

“Well there was an article about the crash, but you could have just read it too.”

“But for some reason, you believe me. You sensed that it was me in the picture.”

“I…”

“It’s okay,” Victoria laughed, “it was overwhelming for me too at first. Enough about me, though. Tell me more about you. All your aunt ever told me was that you were some hotshot photographer in LA.”

A bead of sweat trickled down the side of the bottle. I watched its slow winding journey down the side of the chocolate brown beer bottle and underneath the space of my fingers.

Photography had always been my passion since I was young. When I was five, my aunt Sheryl had bought me a camera after she had entrusted me with taking pictures on the family vacation. Putting a disposable camera in the hands of a five-year would typically result in blurry and off-centered pictures of random animals, close-ups of fingertips and attempts at taking pictures of themselves. To my aunt's surprise when the footage was developed, the pictures I had taken were clear and precise. I still remember the focus I had while taking the photos, my tongue stuck between my teeth as I lined up my subject and waited for the perfect moment to press the button. Since that trip, photography had become my life's work. My father had helped me create my own business when I was a teenager. Instead of weekends spent at sleepovers and tournaments I was instead hosting family photoshoots and graduation pictures for the people in the classes ahead of me. By the time I was sixteen I had earned enough money to buy my own car for my birthday.

The off white 1998 Ford Escort wasn't anything to brag about, but it had gotten me from point A to B until it failed me during my sophomore year of college. Fond memories still fill my mind of scorching hot summer days spent with the winds down trying to get some form of cool air circulating in the overheated metal box. Some of the worst times were at the end when the only way to keep Essey from overheating was to continually run the heat on full blast regardless of the temperature outside. I had come up with the name Essey because my 16-year-old self wasn't as creative or well-rounded as I am now. My logic was simple. It was an Escort, so Essey seemed like a fitting name. Despite the difficulties and nearly insufferable days trying to stay cool in the 100+ Georgia heat, Essey was a memorable car.

If I think hard enough, I can still see her in my mind. The way the thin material of the roof began to bow away from itself, creating a massive fabric bubble when the wind whipped through it from the windows. I can still remember the grasshopper jerky stuck between the crevice in the back windshield because we were never able to find anything thin enough to remove the creature. I still remember the gurgle of the gas tank that was what I felt ill-placed beneath the back seat on the driver's side. But the thing I remember most was the adventures. Essey was responsible for taking me to numerous photoshoots and carrying equipment that in hindsight I believe was too much for her. She had seen beautiful places with me, from beaches to mountainsides I was afraid we would slide backward down.

I recounted this information to Victoria as she sipped on her beer, her eyes shone back at me with an unnatural brightness.

"I went to college for photography and paid my way through with scholarships and the money from my business. I wanted to go to Yale but ended up at UCLA instead," I explained, "I just like taking pictures I guess...but Sheryl always told me I had the gift of…"

"Perspective," Victoria finished before I could say anything else.

I nodded and finished off my beer, sitting the bottle down with a faint clink that seemed to echo around the entire bar. Victoria stared at me as we sat in silence and I shifted uncomfortably, not from her but the creeping feeling making its way up my neck. I tried to shake it off and chalk it up to nerves from all the craziness I had endured from the past few days, but the voice was there again in my mind telling me something big was about to happen.

"I don't like being caught up in things you know. I try to stay away and just observe. Curiosity killed the cat, right?" I stammered, my fingers rapping against the countertop.

"But satisfaction brought it back," Victoria smiled, patting my hand again, "look I understand that it's hard and scary, but being a child of Persephone is also a gift."

"Sure doesn't feel that way right now," I sighed, stretching, trying to relieve the tension sitting in the back of my neck.

"Tell me about Ray," Victoria said calmly tucking a piece of hair behind her ear.

"What?" I frowned, the foreboding feeling in my neck growing.

"You were mumbling that name on the plane. Who is he?"

"I...I don't know, really. It's just a dream that I keep having."

"Tell me."

"I don't remember all of it."

"Tell me what you can remember."

I stretched again, my back cracked with a satisfying pop, but the feeling that something was coming was still there.

I began having the dream about Ray three months ago. At first, I had assumed that I had seen the story somewhere or loose references to it in an article or a post on social media, but the dream had persisted and grown as the months went on. The dream always began the same way with me sitting on a porch staring out at the yard in front of me. There's a storm coming over the hills, and I'm watching the clouds roll in. Leaves are racing across the yard as if they are running from the approaching storm. A flame-haired woman with green eyes comes around the corner of the house and smiles at me. She leans down and kisses me on my cheek and whispers that she loves me before sitting down in the rocking chair next to me. The storm grows closer, and the thunder is so loud that I can feel the vibrations in my chest. Right after the first crack of lightning splits the sky the rain breaks from the clouds and pounds against the house. The wind is whipping the rain around us as we watch the storm from our chairs. Another bolt of lightning dances across the sky and I'm drawn to it. I always found it absurd that moths were attracted to bright lights, but as I watch the tendrils cross the sky I understood them. I step off the porch, and my boots are sinking into the mud as I make my way across the yard to surround myself by the lightning. Suddenly a lightning bolt streaks through the sky and strikes a tree in the yard, setting the wood ablaze. Flames illuminate in my eyes for a few moments before the tree is extinguished by the rain, smoke rising from the singed wood. Curiosity flits through my body, and I get an indescribable urge to touch the tree. From behind me the woman calls my name, fear in her voice. I ignore her and keep walking towards the tree because by this point I am determined to touch the bark that is still flickering red with heat from the sky above. The woman calls out to me again, this time she's screaming, and I turn towards her, but I feel a pulse rip through my body.

"That's usually when I wake up," I sighed finishing the story, the phantom feeling of electricity across my skin is there even as I just recount the dream.

"Is it exactly the same every time?" Victoria asked, her gaze shifting to look over her shoulder.

"No. The part I told you stays the same, but sometimes there are flashes of other things. Once there was a part where I was running through a cornfield chasing a little girl with bright red hair. Sometimes I try to force myself to stay asleep after the pulse, but then the thrum of electricity turns into pain, and I jolt awake."

"You are indeed a child of Persephone Ky. The dreams are the first indication."

"I don't want to be a child of Persephone. I don't even know what that means."

"You have no choice. You read the first notebook. You have taken on Sheryl's charge."

"The notebooks? The story didn't even make sense…"

I trailed off when I noticed Victoria was no longer listening to me and was instead focused on the group of people who had just entered the bar. All of them wore gold torch pins affixed to their chests; the woman from earlier was with them as well. Victoria shifted to face the TV screen instead, her leg bouncing against the bar underneath her feet. The group sat down at the opposite side of the bar from us, their heads hunched in hushed conversations between each other. I watched as they pretended not to watch our every move. Victoria waved over the bartender from earlier and ordered a shot of tequila. Once she got the glass she slammed it back and grabbed my arm dragging me out the door past the group who turned to follow us immediately after. Once we were out the door, she dragged me over to the car and put the keys and a folded note in my hand.

"Go and don't look back," Victoria whispered, "best of luck, my sister."

I remained frozen in place, watching as the group from earlier stood off to the side, the glint of guns showed in their waistbands against the lights of the streetlamps overhead. Victoria shoved me into the car, her fingers shuddering for a moment as she slammed the door. I watched as she mouthed go and took a long breath, her gaze stilling into a mask of calm as she turned and began walking towards the group. I dropped the keys between the seats, scolding myself silently for being like the people in horror movies I always scolded for their clumsiness. Outside the car I could hear the people beginning to chant.

"Etiam mors necesse mori," they chanted, their eyes glowing yellow as the streetlamp next to them slowly dimmed.

Their voices echoed in my head, the same white searing pain from the cemetery. Pain throbbed behind my eyes as I blindly reached around the seat for the keys. My fingers closed over the cool metal, and I scrambled to crank the car, my vision filling with tears as the people continued to chant. Just as suddenly as the pain began it ceased as Victoria began to speak softly.

"I am at peace; my work is done," she smiled.

The car roared to life, and I pulled away from the curb. In the rearview I watched Victoria crumple to the ground, and a gun being tucked away underneath a coat. I turned back towards the road, blindly driving for a while down short streets that ended in dead ends.

9

The sight of Victoria's lifeless body on the ground remained engraved in my mind as I drove. Her final words played like a scratched CD drowning out the hardcore rock I played over the radio. Screamo music blared through the speakers, my mind trying to find purchase on the lyrics instead of the thundering of my pulse and the urge to cry. I knew I couldn't go to a police station or they would dismiss my claims like the Coverton force had done. Instead I kept driving until I became lost and ended up in an abandoned shopping mall. I put the car in park and leaned my head against the headrest with a thud. As my eyes closed all I could see was Victoria's body falling to the ground. I opened them quickly and instead focused on the feel of my jacket under my fingers. The scratchiness of the denim, the wad of what I assumed to be an old receipt in my pocket, and a folded piece of paper. It was at that moment that I remembered the paper that Victoria had shoved into my hand along with the keys.

1472 Maple Grove

Huffinville, OH

I had never been to Ohio, but something about the address seemed distantly familiar. I plugged the address into my GPS and began making my way down the darkened streets once more. Endless stretches of road passed without a single porch light or streetlamp. On any other day the solitude and nothingness would have been a welcome relief from the hustle of my daily life, but now the darkness only held secrets and people who were willing to kill over the nonsense my aunt had scribbled in a few notebooks.

Slowly the markers of civilization returned, and I could see the flicker of lights in the distance. Breaking forth from the nothing loomed a towering, rusted metal bridge. Nestled into the crook of its arches that had stood the test of town were small flickering Christmas lights. I slowed, my eyes focusing in on the small lights that danced along the wrought metal creating a warm contrast to the otherwise eerie bridge. Unlike other bridges I had crossed, this bridge did not boast a thriving lake or fish-filled body of water. Rather it covered a dilapidated network of old warehouses and plants like a funeral shroud. It encased what I assumed was once a small city full of life and wealth, but now the only thing that remained were the skeletons of buildings and the silence left behind when life is extinguished. I listened for the sounds of the bridge groaning against the weight of my car, the guttural sigh being the only sound other than the hum of the car under my grip. The bridge soon faded behind me, a looming mass in my rearview mirror.

Minutes later and just as ominous the downtown buildings of a city came into view. As I slipped into town under cover of night, a dark shadow loomed on my left side. My eyes instantly went to the massive building that had caused the shadow standing watch over the roadway. I couldn't contain the huff that escaped my lips as I noticed the gilded gold lettering over the door of the building that labeled it as the community mausoleum. The bricks of the building were stained dark with time as vines raced up the side of the building in an attempt to reclaim the space back into the land that it was built upon. I wondered what kind of town this was that welcomed you with a monument to death. The walls pay daily homage to the cries of families and loved ones missing the presence of the soulless shells that now lie entombed in the stone walls forever. My family was raised in the traditional southern Baptist ways, except for Sheryl who believed in reincarnation and past lives. I still remember her rambles about past lives and deja vu, which probably led to the notebooks that now sat heavy in the satchel on the passenger seat. Her obsession with coincidences probably led her to create the stories that now rested in the pages. An obsession that the strangers I had come across and the people murdered in the cemetery seemed to share. I shrugged off the chill that raced down my spine and focused on the road ahead as it led me out of town and back into the endless expanse of fields.

Night gave way to morning and with it, the fear that had bubbled low in my gut all night gave way as the once dark fields sprung to life in a wash of bright yellow. Among the butter-yellow fields sat a small house that even in the barely-there light of the morning hummed with life. The house was made for a family. The evidence of that shone in the two-car garage and miniature garage built for the children to park their toy vehicles. A little girl her hair whipping out behind her swung on a swing set anchored to the massive oak tree in the side yard. Her feet rocked back and forth propelling her forward where she could see a view of the world with each arch. A gleeful smile spread across her lips as she looked out at the field of hay, and I wondered what thoughts were going through the girl's mind. Did she look out at the fields and long for what lay beyond the endless rows, or was she content with being on the swing watching the world change around her?

I continued past the house and the girl on the swings to a short dirt road. The lush fields teeming with life gave way to a nearly barren stretch of land. Sitting solitude in the middle of the fields was a small green-paneled house. A flash of one of the inconsistent parts of the Ray dream came into my mind. I was standing on a porch almost identical to the one in front of me, listening to the small red-headed girl on the step in front of me read from a weathered storybook. My fingers tightened on the wheel as I drew closer to the house. Faint flashes of what felt like memories poured into my mind: tending the fields that now lay desolate, kicking up dirt in the cleared out patch in the side yard with the red-headed girl and her friends, carrying the red-headed woman over the threshold. I rolled down the window, hoping the cool air would settle my mind and help me refocus.

Light began to flicker over the ground as the sun rose behind the homestead, sending tendrils of orange and yellow light slicing through the shadows. Although fear still sat in my gut I continued up the drive. In the low light of the morning I could now see a barn to the side of the property. Its doors were faded red like a toy firetruck left out in a storm. I parked the car and made my way over the grounds, my feet kicking up little puffs of dust with every step. Another flash of the dream came racing back to me: a pair of little boot-clad shoes racing through the dirt, joyful squeals spilling from the girl's lips as I chased after her growling like a monster. I made my way past the barn its doors hanging loosely from its hinges. A few leftover pieces of dried hay hung from the windows and littered the yard. The splintered wooden stairs groaned as I made my way up onto the porch and sat down in one of the worn rocking chairs — another flash of what felt like memory took over. I was sitting in this same spot rocking the little red-girl to sleep; her soft snores caressed my ears as I pressed a gentle kiss to the top of her head. A pair of pale arms wrapped around my shoulder copying the kiss I had just placed atop the girl's head.

"Can I help you miss?" a timid voice spoke, ripping the memory from my conscious.

Before me stood a woman a little taller than me, her bright red hair was tied back in a wind-swept bun; paint stained overalls hung from her thin frame. I couldn't place it but something about the soft smile on her lips and the way the morning light danced in her eyes seemed familiar.

"Um...a friend of mine gave me this address. She was supposed to meet me here," I lied, stammering over my words.

> "Right. Well, she must have written it down wrong, nobody stays here but me and my dog."
>
> As if waiting for her cue, a black and brown german shepherd trotted from around the side of the house. She panted, making her way up to sit next to me on the porch. I reached down and scratched between the dog's ears; a happy growl rumbled from her belly. Once I

stopped petting her she sniffed at the red-headed woman's leg then went in the door.

"Sorry. I'll be going then," I stepped off the porch just as a roll of thunder raced across the sky.

"Where are you headed next?" she asked, staring out at the dark clouds making their way over the horizon.

"Toledo."

"Not in that storm. You ever drove in the snow?"

"No."

"Then you're definitely not going. You can stay till it lets up."

"Abigail," she said, extending her hand.

"Ky," I said, shaking her hand and fixing a smile on my face.

With a sweeping motion, she invited me inside; the door clicked shut behind us. Nodding, the woman disappeared into the house, leaving me surrounded by faded family photos and trinkets that only held sentimental value for the people that lived there. My eyes were drawn to one particular picture of a family in the center above the fireplace. Specifically, the man in the center drew my attention, his dark black hair and deep brown eyes sent a shiver down my spine. It wasn't the kind of fear you get from haunted houses but the kind you get from seeing old pictures of yourself and realizing how your life is ticking away. My fingers traced over the glass in front of the photograph recognizing the red-headed woman from my dreams. The little girl standing between the man and woman could easily be a younger version of the woman in the house.

"That's from when I was younger, " the woman's voice cut through the silence as she returned to the living room.

"Have you always lived here?"

"All my life. This farm belonged to my father. I inherited it when my mother died."

"What about your father?"

"He died when I was young. He got struck by lightning during a nasty storm," she sighed, handing me the pillow and blanket she had grabbed from the other room, "he was a good man. I remember playing tag with him in the yard and reading out on the porch. He even tried to save a junkie's life once, but the man ended up dying."

"He sounds like an amazing man," I swallowed hard, a warm feeling that I can only describe as pride crept up my spine.

Thunder rolled across the sky, shaking the eaves of the house. I turned to look out the window, my eyes going wide as I watched the tumult of snow just outside the porch.

“It’s even prettier at night. Feels like being in space.”

“It was just sunny.”

“Welcome to Ohio.”

Our laughter filled the room as we settled down in the living room. She lit the small fireplace underneath the TV and went back into the kitchen. A few minutes later, she returned with two steaming cups of hot cocoa. The warmth from the cup seeped into my cold fingers, my mind momentarily flashing back to the morgue and the feel of Sheryl’s fingers under my own. I shook my head, focusing instead on the toasted marshmallows bobbing in the mug.

“Toasted? I thought I was the only one that did that,” I smiled, taking a long slow sip of the chocolate.

“It’s the way my dad used to make it.”

Pain shot through my head, making me slam my eyes shut as a flash of what felt like memory came racing back. I was in the kitchen with the little red-headed girl toasting a marshmallow on the end of a knife.

"I like cooking marshmallows because it's okay if they are a little burnt," I mumbled under my breath.

"What?"

"Oh. It's just something that came to mind. I'm not much of a cook."

"Funny. My dad used to say the same thing is all."

The couch groaned underneath me as I shifted in my seat, an unshakeable feeling of familiarity crept up my spine. As she continued to talk the feeling grew with each memory of her father triggering similar memories of my own. Putting up a Christmas tree in the corner by the fireplace, lifting her to put the angel on top of the tree and leaving milk and cookies on the small coffee table. A ring had formed in the wood from sitting the cold mug of milk in the same spot every year. I remembered devouring those same cookies while snickering with the red-headed woman in the picture after putting all the presents under the tree, and eating apples and popcorn while sitting on the porch.

I listened to each one of her stories, a smile on my face at the warmth that they began to build in my heart. Outside the onslaught of snow continued to rage, piling up in perfect domed piles in the yard and shrouding the landscape in white powder. Daytime slowly faded into night, and I remained inside with the strange woman that also seemed familiar. Night fell around us, and I was still stuck huddled under a blanket in the old house that groaned underneath the weight of the snow building on top of it.

"I spent my entire life looking for a love like my mom and dad had. Guess I'll never find it," the woman smiled, putting up the family photo album she had been showing me.

"There's time," I tried to encourage her.

"No. My dad always said that when he first met my mom, he knew from the moment they spoke for the first time," she sighed sadly, "I'm off to bed. Let me know if you need anything."

Before leaving, she tossed another log into the fireplace, the wood spit and crackled amongst the flame. I smiled at her wanting to dissipate the sadness in her eyes but not knowing exactly how. Her bedroom door clicked shut moments later, leaving me with only the sounds of the fire and the creak of the old house. I hunkered down underneath the blanket, a satisfied groan leaving my lips as I stretched out. From somewhere in the house, the dog returned and laid down on the floor next to me. There was no logic to the way I felt at the moment, but here in this home I felt safe. Although I felt peaceful and safe for the first time since I left LA for Coverton, sleep still evaded me. For a while, I stared at the ceiling hoping that the monotony of the action would cause sleep to find me, but my efforts proved fruitless. Instead I pulled the second journal from the bag that rested against the couch and began to read.

Life 2: Animal 2

(Parasteatoda tepidariorum)

In my second life, I was born into darkness again. This time the void of nothingness that surrounded me felt like a prison rather than the haven it had been before. As I waited for the light to come, I sat afraid but not knowing why at the time. Images of phantom beasts lunging into the darkness to destroy me played in my mind on a constant loop. On occasion I would feel something touching my skin, poking, and prodding at me as if testing to see if I were alive and breathing. I soon learned that the poking was from my mother and that the lingering warmth I felt against my skin was her. As I waited in the darkness, I took comfort in her warmth until that day when I would see the light again.

After what seemed like an eternity, the light finally returned, and with it a surge of fear when I realized that my mother was gone. I waited for her for a few days, and she returned once her eyes unfocused as if she did not recognize her offspring. When she left again, I took comfort in the knowledge that she was not far, even if she didn't remember who I was. With a sudden surge of courage, I stepped out into the world once more to seize the freedom I had been given.

The world around me was not as slow as before. On the contrary, everything seemed to pass by in a blur around me. I made my way down a long white road until I reached the raging river at the end of it. Tentatively I tried to make my way around the river, but a sudden burst of water sent me end over end down the frothing trail. I gasped my body curling in instinctively to protect myself as the river took me away. Moments later, the water calmed, and I was able to pull myself onto the shore. My body felt heavy as I stopped to breathe for a moment and stare down into the small pond that the river fed. It was then I saw it.

The creature from my nightmares. Its sizeable brown body glistened back at me; fangs bared ready to strike. I slammed my eyes shut and waited, but the pain never came.

Slowly I opened my eyes again, and the creature was still there. I screamed, and the beast screamed with me. I jumped back, and it disappeared into the water. I took a moment to breathe before looking into the water once more. The creature reappeared but only continued to stare. I opened my mouth to speak, and the beast did so as well. It was at that moment that the realization hit me. I was now the creature from my nightmares, long fangs, and wide orb eyes.

Fear came crashing over me like a wave as I thought back to my dream. I had been killed by a beast; now, I had become one. Did that mean I had to kill others? I walked away from the pond through the tall green space; my mind focused on what to do next. I did not want to hurt anyone, but a feeling in my gut told me I would. If I killed others I was no better than the savage beast that brought about my demise.

I wandered in the great green space for days, drinking from the orbs of water that collected on the towering green blades above me. I slept underneath a smooth, hard place, watching the night come to life around me before giving way to the beautiful dawn. I had not taken much except a few pieces of other insects that had already been killed. It satisfied my hunger, but my body also longed for something else that I could not decipher yet.

One morning as the heat of the sun warmed the smooth, hard place; my skin began to itch. Whenever I tried to move my skin protested and tried to break away. The itching grew hour by hour and day by day until I could no longer resist the urge to press my back to the hard space and scrape off the oppressive layer of my body. I rubbed and shook until finally, I felt free once more. I turned to continue on my journey but stopped short when I saw myself staring back. I circled the remains of myself, softly touching it with one of my feet. It crumbled under my touch.

"Am I dead?" I wondered aloud as I stared at my shell.

I stayed there next to it for a few days, my mind spiraling, and my body felt tired and vulnerable. I thought it would be best to keep hidden. After a few days, I kept going leaving the piece of myself behind. The itching happened again, and each time another part of me was left behind, marking the progression of my journey to a destination, I had not yet realized. I felt bigger and stronger each time I left a part of me behind and convinced myself that I must be dead.

After a few years on my journey, I crossed paths with some of my brothers and sisters, but just like our mom, their eyes did not show any recognition. My entire life I was surrounded by passerby whose presence meant nothing to me:

the man with long spindle-like legs, the woman with the red and black polka-dotted coat. But now seeing that I was a nobody in the world of my family made me realize that I was truly alone for the first time.

The loneliness was only made worse by the growing hunger in my gut. A hunger that made every passerby seem desirable, and I wanted nothing more but to feed.

Soon I began spinning webs, a newfound and perfected skill that I had come across as I rested underneath another hard, smooth place. From my resting area I watched as flies flew to and from a dying carcass and I became green with envy. I longed for the freedom that their wings provided, but I could not quite place why their wings also felt like a curse that is not recognized until it was too late. The next morning I ventured out to explore more of my world and came across a tall structure of wood. I made my way inside through a small hole that I assumed the inhabitants of the dwelling had created just for me. Once inside I made my way around other pieces of furniture, or at least that is what the giant people called it. For some reason the giant people struck fear in my heart so I kept out of their sight as much as I could and only moved in the cover of darkness and shadow. I found a darkened corner where I spun a beautiful web and hunkered down for the night. My stomach raged and growled against me as hunger set in once more. I fell asleep but was awoken sometime later from a buzzing sound close to where I slept. My eyes opened to a fly struggling in my web. Its wings beat against the thin lines I had spun, but with each attempt its wings only held fast tighter until it was fully entangled. The hunger returned in a surge of energy, and I found myself making my way down the web towards the struggling creature. As I approached its eyes grew larger, and I could see myself reflected in its numerous orbs. For a moment I paused, the fear in the creature's eyes brought me up short as I remembered a dream I had of being in its place. I stopped only inches away; fangs bared questioning my decision.

"I'm sorry," I whispered aloud as I lunged forward and sank my fangs into the fly's body.

I felt its body go limp underneath me. Its death filling my body with the nutrients I had denied it for so long. I slept the rest of the night with a full belly and a new understanding. For me death was a necessity if I wished to live.

The following morning I awoke early before the time that the giants were generally about. I made my way down the wooden pieces I had climbed the day before but stopped when I felt that I was not alone. I looked up into the eyes of a giant, their eyes full of fear. I paused confused how a creature as large as the giant could be afraid of someone as small as I. I took a tentative step towards it and it ran away, shouting about a spider. For the first time I had a name for what I was, and I sat stunned in the realization that all creatures were afraid of me. I continued on my journey for a bit before encountering another giant who had tracked me down after hearing the terrified yells of the other. I looked up into their eyes, and instead of fear there was what I would come to know as disgust. Suddenly the giant lifted a flat piece on its foot. I jumped to the side dodging the piece.

"Silly giant," I thought aloud.

The giant followed the motion stomping the flat piece down near me as I jumped away. It was quite an entertaining game. The final time I could not jump away, and the giant's flat piece crushed one of my legs. I stared up at the giant, my eyes wide as the flat piece came down again and darkness took over once more, and at that moment I understood that fear is a powerful force when on the giving or receiving end.

A yawn pulled past my lips as I continued to flip through the notebook. Similar to the first one, nonsense diagrams about spider anatomy and life cycles filled the rest of the pages. There was also an Alabama address written on the back of a picture of a log cabin. I snapped the notebook closed and tucked it back into the satchel with the rest of them. For a moment the golden symbol on the front seemed to glow causing me to blink and shake my head. When my gaze fell on the satchel again the glow was gone. Another yawn filled the now silent space. I slid down onto the couch and tucked the blanket around me, allowing sleep to claim my tired body. That night I had the Ray dream again, but this time it was intermingled with the memories Abigail had shared with me.

Hours later, my eyes flickered open as the smell of frying bacon reached my nose. I rose from the couch, shuddering as my feet touched the cold floor. As I stretched, my body popped, the muscles I had been holding so tight unwound. I joined Abigail in the kitchen for breakfast where the woman had laid out an entire spread of bacon, pancakes, grits, and eggs that reminded me of childhood breakfasts. Saturday mornings would bring a breakfast spread like this one along with cartoons on the couch with my father. It had taken some convincing for my mother to serve breakfast in the living room, but my father's bright smile had a way of changing mother's mind. The early morning breakfast and subsequent nap immediately after tucked into my father's arms were among one of the many things I missed about him. We connected over the memories of our fathers for a while before I said goodbye and ventured back outside.

A blanket of snow cloaked the world outside. I trudged through the boot deep snow to the car that Abigail had already cleaned off. Cold crept through the shoes I was wearing. I rolled my eyes at myself and how ill-prepared I was for the cold. The farmhouse was now picturesque in the low light of the morning that glinted off the snow. I cast a final look backward to the step where Abigail stood, her eyes fixated on the singed tree that sat on the edge of the property. Snow rested on the darkened wood, unable to wipe clean the memories made there. I had not noticed it when I arrived, but underneath the tree sat a small stone memorial. It was too far for me to see the name written on the stone, but I assumed it was for the father Abigail remembered so fondly. Staring at the stone sent a shiver racing down my spine. I turned back to the road and continued on my journey towards the airport.

On my way, I passed the same house where the girl had been swinging before. It now set cloaked in a foot of snow, and there was no sign of life outside. The blanket of snow suffocated the once yellow fields, the life of the growing crop momentarily halted until nature ran its course. Seeing the homestead that was once thriving with life in this state was hard to stomach. I wondered what the little girl would think when she came outside later today to swing. Would she find the new landscape calming and signs of a new adventure or would the bleakness of it all seem dreary even in her young mind?

10

I savored the lack of adventure, mystery, or chaos as I arrived safely at the airport. As I waited for my flight I searched for any traces of Victoria's story in the news, but there wasn't a single mention of any shootings or anything out of the ordinary except a prediction for another round of treacherous snowstorms in the coming days. Without incident I boarded my flight and hunkered down into the safety of the window seat. My gaze felt unfocused as the plane lifted above the clouds. Looking down at the perfect boxes of fields below made me long for the homestead and the woman I had just met. I shook off the feeling and began a search on my phone. In my scrutinous studies of the notebooks, the name Persephone was written on the last page of each one. A faint memory of the name mumbled in a high school class came to mind, but I could not recall her story. Upon searching her name I found a plethora of articles, choosing one I began to read as the plane hummed underneath my cheek pressed to the window.

Keeping it in the Family

Persephone was the goddess of vegetation, in specific grain, in Greek mythology. She was the offspring of siblings Zeus, the god of the sky, and Demeter, the goddess of the harvest. Persephone was often depicted as a beautiful goddess whose beauty in the tale of Adonis was thought to rival that of Aphrodite, the goddess of love. Persephone's beauty drew the attention of many gods, but each of her would-be suitors was dissuaded from their attempts by her mother. Persephone was also seen as a representative of a maiden, and her image could not

be sullied. This image changed when her uncle Hades, the god of the Underworld gazed upon her beauty.

Despite Demeter's attempts, Hades continued to pursue Persephone and one day while the goddess was frolicking in a valley, Hades arose from the underworld in his chariot and abducted Persephone. No one was aware of Hades's deed except for Zeus, who did not want to meddle in the affairs of the underworld as that was his brother's domain. However, at the disappearance of her daughter, Demeter became distraught, and the people of the world began to suffer. Demeter continuously searched the world for her daughter; her torch held high above her head as she searched. The goddess continued to search for her offspring until Hecate, the goddess of wilderness advised Demeter to seek council in Helios, the sun god who saw all. Helios upon hearing Demeter's cries admitted that he had seen Hades abduct the girl which sent Demeter into a rage. Helios also admitted that Zeus had witnessed the kidnapping as well.

Upon hearing this news and in a rage because of Hades's actions, Demeter decided to take her anger out on the world until a solution was reached. The land dried up and produced no crops; animals and humans alike died from lack of food. The famine spread across the land and left a shadow of immeasurable misery upon the people. In response the people called out to the other gods and goddesses for help. Unable to answer the cries of their people, the task of appeasing Demeter fell upon Zeus. Seeing that Demeter's rage would cause humanity to perish, Zeus decided to mediate a conversation between Demeter and Hades.

The compromise agreed upon by the god and goddess was simple. Persephone would be allowed to choose her fate. She would be asked if she wished to stay with Hades or return to the surface with her mother. Upon hearing this, Hades devised a plan to keep Persephone as his wife. Since her abduction, Persephone was devastated and cried all day and night. Hades convinced his new bride to consume the seeds of the pomegranate which was known as the food of the Underworld. With each seed consumed the consumer of the fruit would long for life in the Underworld and no longer miss the world above. Persephone ate the fruit given to her by Hades for several days before the meeting with Zeus.

During the meeting with Zeus, Persephone was asked where she would like to dwell. In response she stated she wished to live with her husband in the

Underworld. Demeter was convinced that Persephone had been manipulated in some way to give such an answer and threatened to destroy Hades and his domain. Her threat did not work and in turn she appealed to Zeus's love for humanity. Demeter threatened to continue the famine until every human perished. Zeus in an attempt to appease both Demeter and his brother, along with avoiding any more fighting came up with a compromise.

The terms were simple. Persephone would spend half of the year with her mother and the other with her husband. Neither Hades or Demeter agreed with the compromise but acquiesced. Following the meeting, Persephone became the rightful Queen of the Underworld and Hades's wife. During the months Persephone spent with her mother, the earth thrived with life and bountiful harvest; however, in the

months when Persephone dwelled in the Underworld her mother would become stricken with grief, and the land would lay barren from Demeter's sorrow. This compromise was the Greek's explanation for the changing of the seasons and to reiterate the natural cycle of death and rebirth.

I scanned a few more articles; each one seemed more absurd than the last. However, each of them referenced the idea of rebirth and renewal. After a quick search I found an article on déjà vu and past lives. I found various posts created by cult fanatics and unreliable sources, but the final article struck a nerve. It read:

Have you been here before?

The fascination with past lives and reincarnation is at the heart of many studies today. Definitive evidence to answer the question of what

happens after death remains undiscovered. Scientists at Famington University have done the unthinkable and attempted to mix the rigidity of science with the whimsy of myth.

In a recent study, researchers at Famington concluded that our beauty marks are scars from our deaths in a previous life. That heart-shaped mark on your shoulder is where a deadly snake bit you in the life prior. The crescent-shaped spot on your side is from being stabbed in a previous life. Researchers reached this conclusion by studying hospital birth and death records of a small town in Indiana. In their studies, many of the newborn babies presented birthmarks in the same locations as the deceased in the town. Scholars at the leading institutions in the nation adamantly deny that the correlation between these events is valid.

Along with their research on birthmarks, their studies also sought to prove the existence of an ancient Greek order tasked with protecting the secret to eternal life. According to their findings, this cult is representative of the Greek goddess Demeter and are responsible for countless sacrificial deaths.

The study has since been shut down, but the list below will provide you with the highlights of their findings.

1. **When reincarnated, you reincarnate as the thing that killed you.**
2. **When you experience a shiver down your spine, someone is walking over your grave.**
3. **Your dreams are memories of the life you had.**
4. **Déjà vu is your new spirit connecting with the remnants of your former self.**

5. **Subconsciously your new spirit avoids locations where your old body once dwelled.**
6. **The location, size, and darkness of birthmarks can be used to determine the cause of death in a former life.**

Famington University released a statement rescinding the university's involvement with the study.

University President Edward Lancaster stated, "The scientists in question have abused the university's trust and have since been removed from the faculty and grounds. Famington will always be a place that supports the pursuit of truth even when the outcome could be unfavorable. We hope that these men find the counseling they need."

Stranger still the article held links to stories of people who claimed to remember their past lives. Most of them contained examples that could easily be denoted to coincidence: liking strange foods from youth, babies that lounge like adults, people who are drawn to a smell. The final link, however, didn't come from a news outlet, but from a man's blog. At first, I assumed he was a fanatic waiting to be proven false like the rest, but as I continued to read, I began to question my previous thoughts.

The man's name was Parker, and he lived in a small town in Baton Rouge, LA. The first few posts on the blog weren't full but rather questions he had posed to a message board.

What causes human eyes to change colors?

Have you ever felt afraid to approach a certain location but can't figure out why?

Nobody responded to his questions, although hundreds had looked at it. The next posts were longer, and one, in particular, stood out, sending a shiver of uncertainty down my spine.

Am I crazy?

Louisiana is full of voodoo and mystery at every turn. It's a fact I have known since I was young, but until now, I kept a healthy distance from it all. Three months ago I began having dreams of about a woman…a priestess. Most people told me that it was normal since I was surrounded by images like that all the time. This woman though in the dream was me. In the dream I am making my way through an old house, and the bangles on my wrist are the only thing I hear in the quiet. It is challenging to walk for some reason, but I trudge through regardless.

Softly I open a door into a bedroom and make my way to the small mirror in the corner. It is then that I look up into the mirror and see a fair-

skinned woman staring back at me. Her face is wrinkled and dotted with dark scars from a source that I don't know. Suddenly a man appears in the doorway, his eyes filled with rage. I see the glint of a knife in the moonlight trickling through the door, and then I wake up screaming and in pain.

Every night for months it was the same dream over and over, the pain in the same place in my ribcage afterward. Ironically I also have a thin dark brown birthmark in that exact place where the pain appears. Each night the dream was the same, but before the man appeared I tried to learn more about my surroundings instead of focusing on the face in the mirror. Once I was able to see a waterfront from the window, a group of men were on the docks loading fishing nets into a boat. The room around me was modest, and small trinkets and jars of herbs sat on various surfaces around the

room. The floor underneath me was hard underfoot and groaned with every step. I hadn't noticed until two months in that I see the man's face before he enters the room. When the dream starts he is downstairs looking for me, and I realized that I could walk fine, but I was trying to be quiet so he wouldn't hear.

I have told countless people this story, and nothing ever came of it but laughter and talks about how crazy I was. Until one day I took it upon my self to learn more. I reached out to an artist and had them create a picture of the face from my dream, under the guise of creating a cover for a book. I had no idea why but I began to feel uneasy about telling people my story. The artist gave me a digital copy of the picture, and I used it to run a facial recognition search. Don't ask how I have access to that technology. The search turned up two similar

matches: a woman aged 50 who lived in Venice, Louisiana, and a woman who died at the age of 78 who lived in the village of Jean Lafitte. The second woman's face was almost an exact match for the woman from my dream.

I delved further into the story of the 78-year-old woman and found out that her name was Penelope Beatrice Sinclair. She was born in October of 1968. The people of her town believed that she was a witch, but respected her none the less. Records indicated that she lived in a small house just across from the pier where her husband worked as a fisherman. The only other information about Penelope was a newspaper article about her death. She was killed by her husband in a drunken rage one morning. He stabbed her once in the ribs and left her to die. Neighbors found her later that day, and the police were waiting for her husband on his

return. Upon seeing the police the man jumped from the bow, the momentum of the boat was unable to stop and crashed into him, killing him instantly. A cemetery in the city was the final resting place of the couple. They had not had any children together, but Penelope had a child from a previous marriage named Frieda.

As I read this article, pain flared in my side, and as soon as I stopped reading it faded again. I found a picture of her husband, Otis Sinclair and upon seeing his face I was filled with a mixture of anger and fear so intense that I had to take a walk. Of course, I could not let the strange alignment of events go, and I made the mistake of taking a trip. I drove down to Jean Laffite with a good friend of mine. As we made out way into the town I was immediately seized with fear. My heart began to thunder in my chest, and I had to pull over to the

side of the road to let my friend drive. The panic never faded and the closer we got to the docks and the house that I had found in my search the more intense it became. I don't remember much after that, but my friend told me later that I blacked out and began chanting in Latin. My friend raced me towards the ER but as soon as we were clear of the dock I came to. Upon waking I felt so afraid still and begged her to get me as far away from the village as possible. Thankfully she listened to my pleas, but as we passed the cemetery leading out to the village a shiver so severe raced down my spine that I could have sworn someone had shot ice straight into my veins. We continued to drive past, and my gaze met a woman's standing in the graveyard. I nudged my friend, but as she looked up the woman faded into nothingness. Neither one of us has talked about what we saw until now.

I found out that the woman's daughter went on to have a fruitful and fulfilling life, and the 50-year-old who came up in the search is Penelope's descendant. I have not formally introduced myself to Henrietta Carter, who lives in Venice, Louisiana but I have driven by her home. Seeing her in the yard with what I assumed to be her grandchildren smiling and laughing filled me with a joy so intense that tears sprung to my eyes.

I do not write this claiming that I am the reincarnation of Penelope Beatrice Sinclair. Instead, I write this as a cry for help. Since visiting Jean Lafitte, I have an unshakeable feeling of being followed all the time. One night as I was walking home a man shoved me on the sideway and called me a child of Persephone. As he walked away his eyes shimmered gold, but I dismissed it as the reflection from the streetlight above us. It has

happened again with others, and I am afraid. If someone out there has answers, please contact me because I fear that without answers I will die in the darkness of my ignorance.

"Passengers, please put away all electronic devices, place folding tables and seats in an upright position, and buckle your seatbelts as we began our final descent into Los Angeles," the flight attendant smiled as the others collected trash.

I locked my phone and stared out the window as the skyscrapers I had called home came into view. The plane slowly descended towards the runway and smoothly landed. I released a breath I had not realized I was holding until the man next to me patted my hand gently. Upon disembarking the plane, I immediately grabbed a cab and headed to the hospital to see my mother.

11

I hopped out of the cab, throwing a rushed thank you over my shoulder as I raced towards the hospital doors. I slowed my step as I entered, realizing I probably looked crazy bursting through the doors when everyone else was calm. As I approached the nurse's station, a sinking feeling settled in my gut before I opened my mouth to speak.

"Excuse me. My name is Khylia Toombs. I'm looking for my mother, Elizabeth Toombs. She was airlifted here a few days ago," I tried my best to keep my voice even and calm.

"Give me just a moment," the nurse smiled politely, "turning her attention to the computer."

As she typed away, I took a moment to breathe and look around the ER. There weren't many people in the ER like there typically were. A young mother sat huddled in a corner with her son who was coughing profusely. The boy was cuddled as tight as he could into his mother's arms despite the growing bump of another baby and the lack of space on her lap for him. An elderly couple sat holding hands across from them, a bright blue balloon with congratulations floated above a pristine white teddy bear that sat on the table between them. Both of them wore bright smiles as they gripped each other tightly.

"Ma'am. I'm sorry, but I don't see her name listed here," the nurse said.

"What? I was told she was here. She was flown from Atlanta," I snapped, my fist slamming against the counter, fear settling into my gut once more.

"I'm sorry. Could it be another hospital in the area? We could find out for you?"

"Please, I need to find her."

After a few more minutes that felt like hours, the nurse turned to me her eyes telling me everything I needed to know. I knew what she was going to say but listened regardless I listened as she told me there was no record of my mother in any of the surrounding hospitals. Angry and frightened, I called Trent. He didn't answer. I called again and again as I hailed a cab to take me home.

Twenty minutes later, the skyscraper that housed my condo complex loomed above me. I bypassed the front desk and made my way upstairs. Normally the soothing jazz they played in the elevator did not bother me, but now as I made my way up to my condo, my throat tight with fear, the music was like drums beating in my head. It felt like my breath continued to hitch as I stepped off the elevator and made my way to my condo. My footsteps thundered around the walls as I approached my door and froze.

When I pressed my palm to the door, it swung open without the key. There was no tingle up my spine like the other times. I pushed the door open further and stepped inside as quietly as I could. The clink of ice cubes in a glass filled the silence as I made my way around the corner. With one final breath, I stepped from around the corner…to find my mom drinking a glass of sweet tea at the island in the kitchen.

"Mom. You're home," I stammered, making my way over to the counter.

"Where else would I be?" she frowned, taking a long sip of the drink in her hand.

"I thought you were in the hospital."

"I flew back before you did."

"They told me you were life-flighted."

"Well, they lied. Stop talking crazy and come over here," she said holding out her arms.

I rushed over and fell into her embrace as she held me tight. A shiver ran down my spine, and I could hear a voice telling me to be careful. I shrugged it off and smiled as my mom pressed a kiss to my forehead. Moments like these were rare now, so I welcomed them.

After changing my clothes, I poured myself a glass of sweet tea and listened to what my mom believed happened. She told me that we were in a head-on collision with another car just outside of the cemetery. Her flight home had left the day before mine, and she had been waiting for me ever since. I nodded along, foregoing telling her the rest of my story for now. I just wanted to forget it all and leave the craziness behind me. Once my mom went to take a nap I went to my office to look over the contract requests I had missed while I was away. I left the satchel of notebooks on the coffee table where I could see them from my desk. I was afraid to part with them after everything I had been through with them so far.

Light filtered through the full wall to ceiling window of my condo, the hustle and bustle of LA beneath me as I logged into my computer. I couldn't help the smile that flickered to my face when the photo from my birthday last year sprung up. My sorority sisters had all flown to LA to surprise me, and we had a bonfire on the beach. It was rare for all of us to get together especially after most of them had kids. I logged onto the computer and found that I only had three requests waiting for the following week. It was rare that I wasn't swamped with work, but I indulged in the times I could relax.

My condo wasn't fancy, except for the office, and I had bought it at a considerably lower price. The landlord of the place had hired me when I first moved out to LA to take pictures at his daughter's wedding. He had been so impressed by me that he offered me the place at a discounted price. I stretched out on the sofa, mindlessly flipping through channels on TV, but I felt restless. Every time the channel changed my mind flicked back to the graveyard and my time in Ohio. Each memory stayed for only a moment before moving on to the next like the shutter of a camera. I couldn't stand it any longer, so I picked up my camera equipment from my office and headed outside.

Sun beat down on me from the window panes of the buildings around me. I stopped for a moment letting the warmth sink into my skin, my face upturned to the sun. Cars whizzed by on the busy street next to me as I made my way further into the city. One of the things I loved about my condo was the small community park nestled amongst the buildings. I made my way into the park, indulging in the simplicity of the life around me. I sat down in the shade of a tree and watched as families milled about me. A few children were playing frisbee with their father, laughing and jumping around. I felt ashamed that it sent a pang of jealousy into my heart. After snapping a few pictures of the kites in the sky and the leaves whirling in the wind, I made my way to the small bridge that overlooked the humanmade pond. Flowers floated along in the water, and I paused to snap pictures of a few before looking out across the water at the people once again. One of the things I loved about LA was that it was easy to disappear amongst the crowd, whereas in Coverton you were always seen and there was nowhere to truly hide. Everyone knew your entire life story and every move you made, especially when you're the daughter of the Police Chief. My eyes scanned the edge of the water, looking for an exciting subject to photograph when my eyes met a man standing at the edge of the water.

Be careful.

The voice was back inside my head as I made my way across the bridge and out of the park. After walking for a few minutes, I chanced a look over my shoulder, and sure enough the man was there, his stare unwavering as if he did not care that I had caught him. I picked up the pace, mumbling excuse me as I passed, trying to keep my distance from the man. Across the street I could see the bright rainbow-colored sign of I Dream of Beans. I crossed the street, my heart thundering in my chest. Hairs stood up on my neck as I sprinted across the street, the sound of the wind chime above the door signaling my safety. Silently I thanked the heavens that the coffee shop was crowded as I made my way to the counter to order.

After I ordered, I glanced over my shoulder, and the man was standing in the window staring at me. I quickly turned back to the barista who was smiling brightly at me, holding out a steaming cup of coffee.

"Ky, I'm so glad to see you," Trent's voice cut through the fog of my mind.

I whirled, nearly dropping my coffee in the process. Trent stood in front of me smiling brightly. Instead of the usual tight shirts, he was wearing a simple button-down and jeans. After taking a breath, I forced a smile onto my face.

"What are you doing here?" I asked, not genuinely caring one way or the other.

"I came to see you and your mom. I was going to head to your condo after I left here."

"Good. You can walk me back home. A man has been following me since the park."

"What, man?" Trent asked, looking behind me to the window.

I turned, my eyes going wide as the window was now empty from the man's presence. I shook my head clear and took a seat at one of the small booths in the back to be sure he was gone before I left. Trent slid into the booth next to me with his cup of coffee. Neither one of us talked for a while and focused on the slowly cooling cups in our hands.

"Why did you lie to me about my mother? How did you get that nurse to lie too?" I asked the question that had been weighing on my mind.

"I wanted to protect you, Ky. I knew that the best way to get you to leave was to make you think your mom was in trouble."

"Or you could have just told me I needed to leave," I spat, "after what happened in the cemetery I wanted nothing to do with that town."

"I'm sorry, Ky."

I huffed and rolled my eyes, taking a long slow sip of the vanilla latte I had ordered. At the moment I couldn't bring myself to look at him and instead stared down at my hands. He reached across the table for me, but I swiped his hands away.

"There are forces bigger than you at work Ky. Remember I told you your aunt was a part of a cult," he whispered, leaning in across the table.

"Yes, but what does that have to do with lying to me about my mother."

"This cult, they're dangerous Ky. They call themselves the Children of Persephone. I was assigned to a task force a year ago to bring down the cult, but until now, I've only had false leads."

"You think my aunt was one of them."

"I know it now. The massacre that happened in the graveyard is proof. The cult is known for performing human sacrifices, mass suicides, and other hedonistic rituals."

"Sheryl wouldn't have been a part of something like that."

“She was Ky. We found evidence, and they were going to come after you. That’s why I had to get you to leave Coverton. I wanted you to be safe.”

I wanted to scream at the top of my lungs and tell him that nowhere was safe for me anymore. I wanted to tell him that the cult had followed me and that I was afraid for my life, but instead I just nodded and finished my drink. Silence fell between the two of us as patrons milled about the coffee shop.

I Dream of Beans had quickly become my favorite spot for coffee when I moved to LA. Not only was the location convenient, but the owners of the shop, Natalie and Nathan had quickly become good friends of mine. Natalie had studied culinary arts in France, where she had met Nathan who was on a backpacking trip through Europe. The two had a torrid love affair while they were both abroad that they believed would lead to nothing afterward. However, upon her return to the U.S

Natalie had run into Nathan again and the rest was history. Nathan came from a wealthy family and financed the creation of the coffee shop, while Natalie made the pastries and chocolates daily. The first time I visited the small shop was at 4 am before heading to a photoshoot and they were the closest shop available. Even though they were closed, Nathan had welcomed me in and made me a cup of coffee.

"I've missed you Ky." Trent finally broke the silence.

"I'm sure you have."

"Awww come on. We were voted cutest couple," he sighed, "I miss those days."

"Those days are behind us now Trent."

"They don't have to be. Remember how we would go to the arcade every weekend. We saved up all our tickets to get—"

"A gaming console," I laughed at the memory.

"Right. It took us how long? Two? Three months?"

"Six. We got the final ones we needed on my birthday, but the console was gone already."

We both laughed at the memory of excitedly scrambling up to the counter only to see the glass case empty. The clerk informed us that it would be months before another one came into the arcade. Disheartened we blew the tickets on stuffed animals and enough candy to last a month. Looking at him now I could remember why I had fallen for Trent in the first place. He was kind and silly, not to mention he had a great smile. But that smile also lined his lies with silver.

"Speaking of high school. You would never believe who I ran into at the airport," he laughed.

"Who? You know I'm terrible at guessing."

"Sara Heard, well she's Sara Pitts now."

"I still can't believe her, and Nate got married."

"Same. You two were inseparable in high school."

"Yeah. Times change, I guess."

"You never told me what happened. The reason she stopped talking to you."

"It's a long story."

"I got a lot of time."

"It's because of what happened at the bridge the night before graduation."

"Go on."

I took another sip of my drink before beginning my story. My hands began to tremble, so I focused on the warmth of the cup in my hands instead of the thud of my heart in my chest.

Blue River Covered Bridge crossed over what used to be an offshoot of the Blue River further up North. The water had dried up a long time ago, and people had used the slope of the river's barren banks as a shortcut ever since. There were stories about the bridge being haunted that dated back to the 1930s ever since gangs used the rushing water as quick disposal of bodies. The bridge itself was stained dark brown in some places and teens had convinced each other it was from the blood of mafia victims. Even if gangs didn't use the bridge, it had always been an area of death. Countless people had died in the rushing water or crashed into dead man's curve just around the bend past the bridge. However, everyone in the town visited the bridge because of the mysteries surrounding it. Then there were the pill bottles. Underneath the bridge someone had strung up a series of pill bottles. My father told me that when he was young there were only a few and they had grown in number over the years. By the time I was in high school the entire underside of the bridge was lined with the small bottles full of notes in an encrypted language and little trinkets. Some of them even held bits of candy, but I was never brave enough to pop any of the treats into my mouth.

As time went on it became a rite of passage to leave something in the bottles. I still remember leaving a message in one of the bottles my sophomore year. I had spent weeks prior developing the perfect message and had settled on "don't keep things bottled up". Sometimes when I think about it, I cringe at the terrible puns I used to make. I had never believed in most of the stories that people told about ghosts and strange sightings at the bridge until the night before my high school graduation.

The day had started like every day before it. As seniors we had been done for the past week and had spent each day split between graduation practice and taking advantage of the discounts at the local diner. The day before graduation had been the same. I slept in until 11 a.m. then met up with my friends Sara and

Brittani. We walked together along the same path we had taken to school for the past four years. All of us were in high spirits because today was the last day of practice before the big show tomorrow. Brittani and I were Val and Sal respectively and chatted about the fear of doing our speeches. We split an order of fries, and chicken tenders at Huge Hen then made our way to practice. Aside from the morning sun shining in our faces and being unable to wear sunglasses practice was the same as usual. How hard is it to stand and sit after all?

The trouble began later that evening when we found ourselves hanging out on the swings at the park. Sara was raving on about how cute Nate was when the streetlamps flickered on.

"Oh, crap the lights are on. I need to go home before I get grounded," Brittani laughed pushing herself off the slide where she had been lounging.

The rest of us agreed as we finally took notice of the shadows making their way along the ground. During the day, the park was warm and welcoming because of the bright orange, butt-burning, static shock-inducing slide in the middle of the playground. Now, as the sun sunk underneath the line of the trees the twisted shadow of the slide seemed to slink across the ground like a snake poised to strike. After collecting our things, we made out way through the woods along the same path we had taken that morning. We passed the rows of perfectly picketed houses that belonged to the wealthier residents of Coverton whose families had thrived from the textile mill that now lay abandoned in the middle of town. After the houses the path dissipated into a wall of trees with a clear path cut through the middle. The winding path led deeper into the woods towards the covered bridge that loomed in the distance. Branches reached for each other across the path, their wooden limbs stretched as far as they could go, but failing in their task. Darkness took over from the remaining trickles of light softly filtering through the dense forest.

As we drew closer to the bridge, cold sweat began to form on my neck. On instinct, my eyes scanned the treeline for an animal or another teen from my neighborhood, hoping to avoid walking alone. It hadn't rained in days, making the leaves dry and crunchy underneath our feet. The continuous sound of the leaves crumbling into nothingness mixed with our laughter as we made our way home. Each of us was excitedly talking about our college plans and boasting about our schools when the sound of a twig snapping in the treeline broke through our chatter. We froze, each of us looking towards the other and down to our feet to find the source of the noise. As I looked behind us once more before continuing on the path, a shadow crossed through the treeline.

"Did you see that?" I whispered, my eyes fixated on the shadow that seemed to stare back at me.

"Come on, Ky," Sara whined.

"Seriously look." I pointed towards the darkness in the trees, turning my head only for a second to make sure my friends were watching.

"I don't see anything. Stop messing around Ky. It's late, and we'll already be in trouble," Brittani said rolling her eyes.

"What do you mean you don't," the words died on my lips when I turned, and the shadow was gone.

A chill raced down my spine as I hurried to catch up with my friends who were a few feet ahead. I tripped and went sprawling, throwing my hands out to brace myself and came down hard on my wrist. I winced, picking myself up off the ground before Sara reached down to help.

"Better keep up ladies or The Hunter will find you," Brittani laughed over her shoulder.

"Shutup Brit," Sara hissed, her eyes darting around the treeline as she helped me walk.

The Hunter was an urban legend in Coverton. It was almost as old as the tales about the bridge. The story goes that a hunter was out with his friends for a hunting party when they came across a beautiful doe. Usually, hunters sought bucks for their antlers, but these men became obsessed instantly with the doe. They watched as the beast carefully walked around a patch of Narcissus flowers before leaning down to nibble at one of the petals. The hunter, who was never given a name lifted his rifle to shoot, but the doe heard the movement and ran deeper into the woods. Every day the hunter returned, and every day he saw the doe, only for it to disappear as soon as he raised his rifle.

The man continued this daily ritual for days, weeks, months, years. His body wasted away until one day he went into the woods and never returned. Police searched for this body for weeks, but the only thing they found was his camouflage hat laying next to a patch of Narcissus flowers. Soon the police gave up, but then the stories began of hikers seeing a hunter in the woods at night. Every description was the same: a man 5'7, shortcut brown hair, dressed head to toe in camo and orange, with bright blue eyes that glistened in the moonlight. Each witness told the same story. The man emerged from the trees and asked if they had seen a doe run by, a rifle raised to fire. No matter how many times they answered him, the man would ask the same question again. By that time, each witness said they ran, leaving the man still asking about his prize.

Nothing ever came of any of the stories and police had searched the woods off and on for years. Once a man was found dead next to a patch of Narcissus flowers, a single bullet to the chest, but that had turned out to be the result of a scorned wife.

Shaking away the thought of the hunter and ignoring the tingle creeping up my spine, we made our way to the edge of the bank. Carefully we made our way down the path underneath the bridge. The bridge from above was eerie enough, but from below is seemed almost majestic. The dark wood towered above you high enough to block out the moon, and if you were quiet enough, you could hear the rush of the other offshoot of the river a half-mile away. We made our way under the bridge, our fingers grazing against the pill bottles suspended overhead. My gaze was drawn to a new one that I hadn't seen before. Instead of the usual see-through orange bottle, it was bright blue with a green cap. I reached up to open it when I ran into Brittani's back.

"Move Brit. I want to get a closer look at this one," I said, rolling my eyes and pushing her forward some.

Brittani whimpered, a sound I had never heard her make in the ten years I had known her. I looked over her shoulder and froze. Standing a few yards away on the other side of the bridge was a man with shortcut brown hair, dressed head to toe in camo. Mud covered his boots despite the dry ground underneath him. In his hands he held a hunting rifle poised and ready to shoot, the metal barrel glinted in the light of the moon from the other side of the bridge. Then there were his eyes. Cerulean blue and shining even in the darkness underneath the wooden slats. He seemed to look past us as he opened his mouth to speak.

"Have you seen a doe run by?" the man asked, his voice hoarse as if he had been talking for quite a while.

"N—n—no sir," Brittani stammered, her hands shaking as she spoke.

"Have you seen a doe run by?" he repeated, his eyes still staring past us.

"No," I said, forcing my voice to sound calm and strong.

I grabbed ahold of Brittani's hand and led her past the man with Sara on my heels. He didn't move and continued to stare at the spot where we once stood.

"Have you seen a doe run by?"

We picked up our pace, leaving the man behind us as we raced towards the opposite bank where the trail ascended once more. As we began to climb the slope, a shot rang out behind us; a scream ripped from Brittani's throat as she sprinted the rest of the way up the bank. The tingle in my neck was back, and I felt an urge to go check out the source, knowing it probably came from the hunter we had seen. Sara grabbed my arm as I turned back, her eyes wet with fear and begging me not to go. I shrugged her off, plastered the best smile I could muster onto my face and walked back towards the bridge. Once I was within eyesight of the bridge once more, I saw the man standing over a deer. Blood trickled from a single gunshot wound in the deer's chest, marring the delicate brown hide. The deer's dark brown eyes stared ahead, as unseeing as the man's. The man finally looked down at the dead deer at his feet then back up to me, before vanishing. A chill filled the air around me, clawing at my throat and making it hard to breathe. I turned and ran for the bank, catching up with Sara and Brittani at the top.

"Did you see anything?" Sara asked, holding Brittani tight.

"No. There was nothing there," I lied.

We made it home safely and vowed not to tell anyone about what we saw. The next day I returned to the bridge in the daylight searching for proof of what I had seen. Dew still clung to the blades of grass along the bank, and the morning birds had not stopped singing yet. I made my way back to the underside of the bridge, scanning the area for blood or footprints, but the only signs of human interaction were already wiped away by the breeze. I ducked underneath the bridge, my eyes immediately finding the blue bottle from the night before. Carefully I unscrewed the cap, a gasp puffing from my lungs as I dropped the bottle and ran. Inside was a single Narcissus flower and a piece of deer hide, still bright and bloody.

Trent's laughter filled the coffee shop, his hand going over his mouth to keep himself from snorting. He waved an apology to the other patrons and feigned wiping tears from his eyes.

"That is the stupidest thing I have ever heard," he snorted.

"It's true," I retorted.

"Sure. You saw a ghost," he took a sip of his coffee, "I don't believe that nonsense."

"It's true, and I couldn't let it go. That's why Sara stopped talking to me."

"Sounds like she stopped talking to you because you're crazy."

I huffed, Trent's laughter was causing more people to look my way. I hated being the focus of other people. Annoyed at his continued laughter, I slammed my cup on the table and walked out. I could hear him calling out to me to come back, but I continued down the street, looking over my shoulder as I walked. Sure enough a few moments later Trent exited the coffee shop and raced down the street to catch up to me.

"I'm sorry, Ky. If you saw a ghost, I believe you. Even you have to admit the story seems unbelievable."

"Unbelievable. Unbelievable," I turned on him, my fists balled at my side, "unbelievable is the presence of a cult in Coverton, Ga. Unbelievable is finding out that my aunt Sheryl was the supposed leader and her cult massacred people in the cemetery during her funeral. Unbelievable is being chased by a cult that I want no part of, but apparently I'm roped into because of some stupid journals I found in the wall of my dead aunt's house! So don't tell me what's unbelievable!"

My chest heaved as I turned on my heel and walked away from him. I heard his footsteps following behind me and turned to stare him down. He stopped short, seeing the anger shining in my eyes.

"Sorry," his final attempt of an apology fell on deaf ears as I continued on my way home.

When I returned to my condo, my mother was fast asleep on the couch, her hand clutched to her chest and tucked under her chin. She was snoring softly, so I tried not to wake her as I made my way across the room. The bag that I had left on the coffee table was open, the notebooks spilling out onto the smooth surface beneath. Anger overcame me for a brief moment followed by fear as I scooped up the notebooks and tucked them under my arm. Once inside my bedroom, I stretched out across the bed. I held the satchel to my chest and closed my eyes, focusing on my breathing. With each inhale I tried to visualize positivity entering my body and with each exhale the negative thoughts and memories from the past days leaving. Usually, this exercise helped some, but today, I could only focus on the weight of the notebooks in my arms. I pulled the first two from the satchel, rolled over onto my stomach and reread them. This time I took my time, searching for any clues to their importance or why they were written in the first place. Finding nothing new I looked over the other five, each one was the same as the last, but as I looked at the last notebook I noticed a drawn sketch in the back, of a deer. The deer's head was wreathed in small yellow flowers. Looking back at the other notebooks, I found the same sketch on the final page of each one. Taking out my phone I searched for Persephone again, my mind vaguely remembering something I saw earlier. I found the article again listing Persephone's symbols including the Narcissus flower and the deer, which was a symbol she shared with her mother. Exhaustion won over, and a long yawn pulled from my lips. I tucked the satchel into bed with me and pulled the covers around me for an afternoon nap. The annoyance of having people chase me because of some myth that I didn’t even believe was exhausting, but I let it all melt away as I fell asleep.

12

Dust kicked up around my feet as I raced behind the younger version of Abigail on the bike a few feet away. Her bright red hair shone in the sunlight, her laughter tickling my ears.

"You got it, Abby! Keep going!" I cheered, slowing down to simply watch the girl smiling and riding her bike without the training wheels for the first time.

"I'm doing it, daddy!" she squealed, eyes bright with joy.

Suddenly storm clouds rolled in, and I watched as fear clouded the joy in Abigail's eyes. With the storm came a wave of darkness that overtook everything in its path, sucking everything down into the waiting raging depths of the underworld below. I raced towards

Abigail who was frozen in place, but no matter how fast I ran I never got closer.

"Abby!" I screamed as darkness enveloped her.

"Daddy," the cry was small, and the last thing I heard before the darkness took me too.

Rain pounded against my bedroom window, almost as hard as my heart pounded in my chest. I ran a hand over my face, wiping away the sweat that soaked my entire body. A cold chill trickled over my body, and I gulped in the air like a man held underwater. Lightning streaked across the sky like fingers reaching out to a forgotten love. I watched as the lightning struck again, this time it was closer to my building, almost like it was reaching for me. I felt myself being drawn towards the window to watch the storm rage outside. When the lightning struck this time, my awe was replaced with fear. I hastily moved away from the window and back into the living room. My mother was in a similar position to where I was before, staring out at the raging storm.

"Mom?" I said softly walking up to her at the window.

"Hey hun," she replied, turning to hug me close.

I snuggled deeper into her arms as we watched the storm rage outside. Another tendril of light snaked across the sky, accompanied by a roll of thunder, making me jump. She laughed and kissed my forehead before guiding me over to the couch. We curled up on the couch together, listening to the rain patter against the windowpane.

"Remember when you were little, and you would hide in that fort in your room until the storm passed," my mom laughed.

"What?"

"Yep. Every time it stormed we would find you in your fort, and at night you would crawl into bed with us."

"Oh yeah, and dad would sing the thunder song," I smiled fondly at the memory.

"Thunder roll, roll on away. You've got to leave cause you can't stay. Thunder, thunder roll away," my mother sang, her eyes closed in thought.

I closed my eyes, listening to the rain and wind outside, enjoying a moment that reminded me of the way things used to be with my mom. Before my father died, my mother and I would have tea parties and stay up on weekends watching movies. Those moments faded into memory once he was gone, replaced by silent dinners and nights alone watching our favorite shows.

"Did you take up journalism or something?" she asked, breaking the stillness of the moment.

"What?"

"The notebooks on the coffee table. I noticed them earlier. The bag is new too, right?"

"Oh. Aunt Sheryl left them to me. They were like a diary for her I guess," I tried to keep my voice calm, even though there was a strange tingle crawling up my neck again.

"Pssh," she huffed, "Sheryl never had nothing good to say so I can't imagine they're worth a read."

I chuckled shifting a little in her arms, making her hiss. Concerned, I looked down to her hand where the tips of her fingertips were brighter pink as if she had been burned. I sat up and shrugged off the blanket she had wrapped around my shoulders.

"What's wrong?"

"How did you burn yourself?"

"This storm has been going on for a while now. I hope it doesn't get worse, but you don't have to worry about floods like we did in Coverton."

“How did you get that burn on your hand?”

“On the stove. How else would I get a burn at home?” she shouted, her brow furrowed, “you’ve been acting strange since we got back from Coverton. You keep asking all these random questions and being suspicious of everyone and everything.”

I curled my fists into the couch as she loomed over me ranting. Anger surged in my veins, at her words. She had no idea any of the trials I had been through. She didn’t know about the attack, the murder I witnessed. Elizabeth Toombs, oblivious as always.

“I’m fine mom. Storms just put me on edge,” I sighed, trying to ease the tension in my neck.

“It’s that town. It changes people for the worse. It killed your father and changed Sheryl. She was always a little strange, but it only got worse over the years. All of a sudden she developed weird obsessions like spiders and drowning. Then there was her anti-drug crusade for a few years. I tried so hard to reach out to her, to understand, and she just shut me out. Like you're doing now."

I swallowed hard, trying to overcome the lump in my throat. Her rant faded into white noise. Instead, I focused on the lightning striking outside and the rain instead of her. I rose to my feet and grabbed my jacket from the back of the chair.

"Where are you going?" she yelled after me.

I ignored her and grasped ahold of the doorknob. Pausing for a moment when I felt the tingle return to my neck. I turned, grabbed the satchel from the coffee table, and walked out the door. As soon as I stepped outside, rain soaked through my jacket, making the material stick to my skin. Thunder rolled overhead as I continued down the street to the small bar a few blocks away. Typically the streets of LA weren't frightening to me, but now with the lightning splitting the sky fear sat heavy in my heart. For a moment I contemplated turning around, apologizing to my mom, and throwing the notebooks away. The thought of tossing the notebooks aside was tempting but also filled me with a deep dread. I made my way through the sprinkle of people hunkered under umbrellas and shop awning to the door of The Wooden Nickel.

The Wooden Nickel was a dive bar that sold cheap, but strong drinks and boasted an old school pinball machine in the corner. The machine didn't work properly. No matter how many times you kicked it or added quarters the machine remained frozen in time, showing the insanely high score some drunk twenty-year-old had gotten twenty years ago. When I was young, my mother would send me off to school or work with the ominous phrase "don't take no wooden nickels". For years I asked her what it meant, and she would promise to tell me when I was older. On my 21st birthday I asked her once again, and she gave me the same response. Wooden nickels according to the search on my phone were novelty coins printed for fairs and festivals. They were only useful in certain locations, but as a whole they were worthless. That was until The Great Depression when select shops allowed them as currency due to a shortage of their minted counterparts. Nowadays wooden nickels only hold value for collectors and those with familial ties to the coin. The bar got its name from the proprietor's father who was a collector of the currency. Written on the wall above the bar was the life motto he had lived by "Everything under the sun has a purpose and a value, even wooden nickels". The bar employed the homeless and those convicted of felonies. It was a place where everyone was given a second chance, just like the coin from which it got its name.

Stepping across the threshold, the first thing I noticed was the soft clink of the broken pinball machine in the corner. It was quieter than normal; the only patrons in the bar were an older gentleman hunched over a flat beer, and a woman soaked to the bone with a leather jacket drip-drying on the back of her chair. I joined the woman at the bar, peeled my jacket from my arms and draped it across my chair. She turned to look at me, her gaze obviously raking along my body. I shifted in my seat, my gaze staring straight ahead to avoid any eye contact with her. I chanced a glance to the side. Sitting on the stools she was slightly shorter than me, and I found myself drawn to the dark red-brown hair draped over her shoulder.

"You're staring," I gulped.

"Yeah because you look like shit."

Nervous laughter burst from my lips.

"Thanks. Are you this nice to all strangers?"

"Just the cute ones."

"I thought I looked like shit," I blushed, thankful more than ever for my darker complexion.

"Touche." she sipped her drink, "start over?"

I held my hand out to her, momentarily indulging in the warmth of her skin in my palm. Along her fingertips were small little callouses, evidence that she played a string instrument. Just above her wrist was the beginning of an intricately woven tattoo sleeve. My gaze scanned along the carefully drawn artwork inscribed into her skin.

"I'm Rose."

"Kyhlia, but people just call me Ky."

"Well, Ky." she smirked, "can I buy you a drink?"

"Sure, a rum and coke, please."

The bartender nodded, returning moments later with my drink. He winked at me before returning to the other side of the bar. For a moment, I just stared at the glass and the beads of moisture clinging to its sides. Without another word, I raised the glass to my lips and downed the drink. Fire raced down my throat from the drink that I'm sure was about ninety-eight percent rum. When I sat the glass back on the table, Rose was staring at me, her cheek propped up on her palm.

"Something tells me you've had a rough day," she laughed.

"That's an understatement."

"Hmm. I'll get you another," she motioned to the bartender.

"I'll have whatever she's drinking," I corrected.

He returned, setting two hot pink drinks in front of us. Rose took a slow sip of hers as I did the same. My brow furrowed at the taste.

"Cosmo?" I questioned.

"Yep."

"Why?" I took another sip before setting the glass down.

"It's the tattoos, right? The reason you're surprised," she sighed.

"What? No—"

"It's okay, Ky. I'm used to it. People see a woman tatted up, wearing leather, and they make assumptions."

"I'm sorry I didn't mean—"

"I'm just messing with you," Rose laughed, "I ordered one to make myself feel fancy. Never had one until today."

Both of our laughter filled the quiet space, and Rose shouted a rushed apology to the man in the booth. Rose, after a few more drinks opened up about herself. After pursuing a degree in graphic design, she had become a tattoo designer. When I asked the difference, she explained that she created sketches and custom pieces but couldn't bring herself to do the work. She had an intense fear of needles. To compensate she had partnered with her college roommate and best friend to open a tattoo shop called Inkling.

"All art starts with an idea," she said, staring into her glass, "it's a glimmer of your true self begging to be manifested in physical form. We try to capture that in every part of the process."

I listened with rapt attention as she continued. As she spoke, she seemed to space out, staring blankly into her glass, and stirring the olive around in her drink.

"Everyone has their medium: ink, words, paint. Mine is pencils."

She turned her arm to reveal a beautiful lily that ran along her forearm. I knew nothing about flowers, so she explained that lilies could thrive in darkness, but it does better with some light. For her the flower was a representation of herself. She was the youngest of three;

the other two were twin boys who had grown up to be lawyers. Both of her parents were politicians and growing up she had felt like she was always in their shadow. Throughout high school her parents had kept her sheltered while continuously encouraging her to pursue a public service career. Like a studious daughter she had done just that until her sophomore year in college. To keep up with her studies, she had begun taking Adderall then Xanax. The Xanax had been her breaking point, and she quickly spiraled into addiction. After a bender on the drugs mixed with vodka and pineapple in a cocktail she called Ambrosia, followed by waking up in the hospital a day later, she decided that she needed to make a change. Much to her parent's dismay she changed her major from sociology to graphic design, but their opinion was invalidated since they hadn't visited her in the hospital or checked in while she was in rehab. After graduation, she had changed her outlook on life, realizing no one should live in the shadows.

I sighed, her words resonated with me more than I would like to admit. Although I was an only child, I was always under the shadow of my father. When you're the daughter of a public servant, you are always under the watchful eye of the community, and in Coverton they were all waiting for you to fail.

"I'm glad you had a turnaround," I said finally coming out of my musings.

"Me too. Otherwise, I wouldn't have met you."

"I don't know if that's a good thing."

"Huh?" she frowned.

I told her everything down to the smallest details: the cemetery, the shadowy figures, cryptic notebooks, Ray, and that I'm pretty sure I witnessed a murder. I even told her about Abigail.

"Do you believe any of it? The past live stuff?"

“I don’t know what to believe honestly. It all seems so absurd, but I can’t shake the feeling that it's true. I’m afraid but not worried if that makes sense. Those notebooks—when I hold them they feel important—like I have to protect them, but none of this could be real, right?”

“Does it matter?” Rose finished her drink and smiled, leaning her cheek against her palm again.

“Real or not it’s one hell of a story.”

A calm settled around me, and I began to feel at ease again. Reverently I ran my fingers over the symbol on the bag before pulling out the third journal. The first page of the notebook had a guitar on it where the animal silhouettes were in the previous ones.

“Do you want to read it with me?” I asked, immediately wanting to take it back as soon as I said it.

"I don't know. I don't want to be possessed by your aunt's ghost or something."

"It doesn't work that way…I think. I don't know how any of this works."

Rose laughed and ordered two beers. Once they were in her hands, she led me over to a booth in the corner. I slid in next to her, grateful for the angle of the booth that gave us semi-privacy. I opened the book to the first page, and Rose slid in closer, her eyes alight with excitement.

"I don't know why I'm sharing this with you," I huffed.

"Sometimes you need someone to talk to or…maybe you just think I'm hot."

I rolled my eyes but turned the page and began to read; Rose's warm cheek pressed against my shoulder.

Life 3: Human 1

In my third life, I came screeching into the world. This time there was darkness for only a mere moment before there was a bright light and the world greeted me once again. I was born on April 1st, 1903 in the heat of a spring day in Georgia. My parents, Jefferson and Collette Scheets were sharecroppers trying to make their way in a world where the odds were stacked against them. From birth I was a trickster, but what would you expect when you were born on the fool's holiday. I spent hours of my childhood finding ways to pad my clothing to protect me from my daddy's belt and rubbing grease on my behind when I was unsuccessful. My father and I always fought because he took me for a fool when the real idiot was him. He had bought into the ideals that were spewed at us during the time, that times were changing. He believed the field of beans he grew under the good graces of the landowner who lived in the mansion down the street, was going to change things for our family. He believed that with enough hard work and a good harvest, we might be able to one day afford a mansion of our own or at least charming farmhouse.

Personally, I think my dad had heard the fairytale about the beanstalk one too many times. I always hated that story, because who really wins? The giant loses his fortune, and you really expect me to believe that a giant fell from the sky and nobody died? Only fools believe in fairy tales if you want something you have to take it. A magical fairy or wizard isn't going to appear out of anywhere to help you out. It didn't help that I couldn't read the stories on my own and had to rely on the short version that changed every time one of my parents told it.

My parents always said I didn't listen, but the truth is I never liked learning things that didn't apply to me. As I got older, my mom tried to send me to school, but after putting a frog in the teacher's desk, I was sent home with a note never to come back. From the time I was born people had their opinions about me. I was the oldest of three siblings. I was also the loudest and most outgoing, a fact that would help me in the long run.

More than anything though people called me lucky. It all started when I was six years old and got bit by a rattlesnake. The creature's fangs were dried up, and I walked away with just the mark on my leg from its teeth. When I was eight, I ate a bad batch of polk salad that sent me running to the outhouse every ten minutes. The same dish killed the little boy I had shared it with. I don't believe in luck; I'm just smart enough to always turn things in my favor. Growing up on the small plot of land I had to hold my own, and I could tangle with the best of the kids in my town.

When my mom started hearing voices and seeing things that weren't there, the boys in the neighborhood would make fun of her and throw rocks at her feet as she sat on the porch. My younger sister had to tend to my bloodied nose and fists whenever the boys got too close, and once I had to get a cast when one of them broke my arm. He had thrown a rock that hit my mom in the forehead, sending a tendril of blood down her face. Seeing the blood snaking its way down her face as she continued to mumble sent me into such a rage that I broke a branch across his back. He had recovered faster than I thought and slammed me to the ground, breaking my arm. I'll never forget the disgusting angle my arm was in before being snapped back into place.

My father died when I was eleven. Henry, the workhorse that had been my father's pride and joy reared up and kicked the old man square in the chest. The doctor said his heart stopped on impact. Mom was the one who found him, but I was the one who found her. She was sitting with his lifeless body in her arms telling him about her day. The coroner said he had been dead for hours. Every day she repeated the routine. I would find her somewhere in the house or outside telling him about her day, eyes glazed over and staring at some spot in the distance. Some days she would ask him about his and smile as if she heard an answer. Others I guess he didn't respond; she would get angry and throw things. On her angry days, I would sit on the floor and sing to her until she calmed down. It didn't matter the song. After a few notes, her fire would fade, and she would sit down, humming along with me. I cherished those moments that reminded me of the woman she used to be. The woman that sang as she swayed along with the other ladies at the shade tree services on Sunday morning and hummed as she knitted at night.

Singing was one of the few things I took time to learn. Singing made sense. It was just words that showed how you truly felt about the ups and downs of life. Music was just as important. Music opens your heart for the words; then the words make you stay and listen. Everyone around town would catch me singing and crooning as I did work around town. Then I turned fourteen. I can't really explain it, but something changed. It was like all the fire left me, and I just didn't feel like singing anymore. My friends took it upon themselves to help me get my love for music back by taking me to Blue River.

Everyone in town had heard about Blue River, but the problem was you never knew exactly when it was held. Blue River or Blue River festival was the name given to the gathering of musicians and artists on either side of the slow winding bank of the river. It was normally held in the middle of the month, but you never knew when because when the beginning was unsure, and no one wanted it to end. Musicians from all over would come to the banks to play and socialize. The first time I went was with my friends Paul and Jerimiah. I didn't have many expectations for what would come of us going but little did I know my life would never be the same after that first night.

Blue River held a series of firsts for me that would shape me as a man. It was the first time I held a guitar in my hands. It was the first time I met Quincy "The Marksman" Martin, and it was the first time I met Marla St. Troy in person.

As we made our way towards the banks, the first thing we noticed was the fires. Their light flickered through the trees like fireflies inviting you deeper into the forest. Once we broke free of the trees the sound of laughter filled our ears. People sat around the fires and outside of tents smoking and drinking. Alcohol was banned, but nobody worried about Coverton, especially during Blue River.

We made our way through the rows of tents, the smell of beans, greens, and chitterlings made our stomachs growl. Since dad died, my younger sister was taking care of all the cooking, but without my mother's guidance, meals were barely edible. I stopped just outside the fire of one tent where an older woman stooped over a large pot of neckbones. She looked up at me smiling before handing me a bowl of neckbones and rice. I smiled back at her and gratefully took the bowl. I found a log to sit on to eat while my friends continued wandering through the village of tents.

Despite the food burning my mouth I kept eating until the bowl was empty except for the bones.

"Thank you," I smiled, handing the bowl back to the woman.

As I stood up again, the loud strum of a guitar broke through the crowd. Everyone turned and began walking deeper into the tent city. Whispered murmurs raced through the crowd as we approached a gray-haired man hunched over an acoustic guitar. The slouch hat that sat atop his head had a moth hole in the brim; his wrinkled, fingers slid down the neck of the guitar with ease as he began plucking away a song.

Well, you know my pockets empty,

My house is empty too, and

There's a place in my heart used to belong to you.

You know I'm weary.

I get so weary all the time.

You know I get weary, baby

The way you runnin' through my mind.

I lost all my money.

What little bit I had.

Then you went and told me

You weren't coming back.

You know I'm weary.

I felt drawn to the older man as his voice carried away on the wind. Everyone around me was just as enraptured as he sang his tale of sorry and heartbreak. My gaze followed the lines of his gnarled hands up to the silver coin that hung limply around his neck. I swallowed down the gasp that tried to escape when I realized that I was listening to the legendary Ambrose Walker.

My father had told me stories about Ambrose or A.W as most people called him. A.W was a former slave who had been the last one to leave the plantation after their freedom was given to them. When he wasn't at the river he was somewhere still playing guitar. My dad would tell me stories about the poor man who would play outside of shops and restaurants for booze and food. Despite A.W's story no one could deny the man's gift.

A.W finished his song and smiled politely at the crowd as a few people dropped coins into the tin can at his feet. My gaze locked with his, and he waved me over with a smile.

"You Jefferson's boy, right?" he asked, spitting a stream of tobacco on the ground next to him.

“Yes, sir.”

“Too bad ‘bout ‘im passin’. He was always off dreamin’.” He pulled a flask from his pocket and took a swig, “if he spent mo’ time learnin’ to break horses he wouldn’a died like he did.”

“Maybe, sir.”

“Nah,” A. W sighed, “he prolly would’a died in the war anyway”

I shrugged, staring into A.W’s eyes were beginning to make me uncomfortable. The light of the fires nearby flickered in and out of his clouding vision.

I sighed, "I ain’t got dreams. I just live life cause it's out of our control anyway."

"That's best. There's only three types of people that dream: chil’ren, idiots, and dead men." He took another swig from the flask in his hand.

Silence filled the space between us as I stared out at the crowd of people dancing and smiling. Each one of them had made their way down to the river for whatever reason: escape from the monotony of life, escape from their spouse, escape from their sadness. I realized we were all here to escape, but I had only just noticed I was running.

"You ever played?" A.W asked, holding out his guitar.

"No, sir."

"Ever wrote a song?"

"No, sir. I don't know how. I ain't got nothing worth saying no way."

A.W shook his head and patted the stump next to him. I sat down, and he lowered the guitar onto my lap. He showed me where to hold my fingers and the basics of plucking out a tune.

"You should feel honored kid, " a voice broke my concentration, "that old man don't let just anyone touch Maggie."

The man handed A.W a bottle of whiskey which was taken gratefully with a nearly toothless smile. A. W cracked open the bottle and took a long pull before taking the guitar from me.

"That there's my son Quincy." He pointed before turning back to the strings.

"I told you to stop telling people that. I don't want to be known as the son of the town fool, " Quincy spat.

A.W took another drink of the whiskey before waving Quincy away. As he turned to walk away, Quincy motioned for me to follow him. For a moment, we just walked in silence. We kept walking until we were just outside the line of tents. He leaned against a tree and pulled a cigarette from his pocket. I watched as he lit it with practiced ease and took a long drag. Smoke billowed up and around his head before dissipating in the wind.

"How's your mom and them?" He puffed.

"Good."

"Stop lying. I heard y'all been struggling since your daddy died. Three years, right?"

I'm not sure why I lied to him. Everyone in town knew my family was struggling to make ends meet. I had picked up a job helping on neighboring farms, but it wasn't enough to keep our land from sinking into bareness. The fields that were once green and sprouting with life now sat brown, being slowly blown away in the wind. Although I knew the truth, I still couldn't bring myself to admit it out loud.

"We good. You heard wrong. Why don't you claim your dad? Everyone loves him."

"Everyone pities him. That string-plucking old fool is delusional. He looks down on people with dreams but ain't nothing wrong with them so long as you can do it."

He held out the cigarette to me. I took it even though I had never smoked before. The smoke burned my lungs, and I did my best to keep from sputtering like an idiot in front of Quincy. A smirk broke out on his face as he took it back.

"He's a liar you know, " Quincy sighed as he finished the cigarette and snubbed it against the tree.

"About?"

"He had dreams once. Dreamed of being a musician. When I was little, he would tell me that someday we would travel the world off his music. The old fool didn't realize nobody wants to hear a tired old man singing about a tired old love."

"He still could."

"It doesn't matter right now. Rumor is, men getting drafted left and right. I could get drafted any day now and I ain't spending time worried about that old fool."

I said nothing but shifted on my feet; my hands stuck in my pockets. My gaze drifted towards the tents and fires a few feet away. I had heard about the draft, and a few of the older boys from the neighborhood had been shipped off already. I couldn't imagine going to war. What would my family do then?

"You listening?" Quincy smacked me on the head.

"What?" I rubbed the stinging spot.

"I asked if you wanted to come work with me. I provide people with the services they need, and I need someone like you."

"What's the catch?"

"Ain't no catch. Look, if you want to help me come to Trudy's one night."

Without another word, he left and made his way back towards the fires. I stared after him for a minute. Earning more money for my family would help of course, but I was wary of working with someone I had just met. Not to mention how vague he described the job. The fast-paced notes of a fiddle drifted through the trees, and I found myself looking for the source of the sound.

As I approached the river's edge, I realized the sound was coming from the other side. The banks of the river were joined by a rickety steel bridge that sat low over the water; its edges were rusted from the water continually lapping at its edges. When it rained the water would swallow the bridge until it resided. It was almost impossible to cross the bridge without becoming mesmerized by the rocking of the water beneath you. I paused, looking down at the water swirling underneath me. It was as if the water was calling to me, almost begging me to sink into its depths. My body lurched forward suddenly, and I felt the water racing up to reach me, but before I could fall into the water, my friend grabbed me by the shirt laughing.

"You okay Billy?" Jeremiah laughed, patting me on the shoulder.

"You almost knocked me in!" I shouted, "you know I can't swim."

"I wasn't going to let you fall in."

"Right." I shrugged off his hand and continued walking towards the music.

On the other side of the river was a large opening that housed a big bonfire in the middle. Off to the side of the fire was a massive tent where a large woman stood hunkered over a large pot. I could smell the chitterlings as we approached. Three pans of hot buttered cornbread sat cooling on a log next to the pot. The fiddle that I had heard earlier was perched on a woman's shoulder next to the bonfire. A few other musicians were scattered around as well, adding to her lilting notes. Around the fire, couples were dancing and laughing. I sat down on a log next to the large woman and stared out at the others dancing around. From among the small crowd of people, a girl came twirling. Her hair was tightly coiled atop her head, but she had a smile that could light a million fires. She had eyes as dark as the mud pit in my neighbor's backyard that the pigs wallowed in during the heat of the day. My heart pounded in my chest as I took a bowl from the woman and made my way closer to the girl.

"Hey," I stammered, holding out the bowl.

She looked down at the contents, turned up her nose, and walked away. I dropped the bowl and grabbed her arm.

"Do you know who I am?" she huffed, pulling away from me.

"No, but I would like to," I smiled.

"I'm Marla St. Troy."

I took a step back recognizing the name. I couldn't believe that the wild-haired girl in front of me was the daughter of the stuck up mayoral assistant. Taking a closer look, I could see it now in the way she carried herself. If we weren't in the middle of a field next to the riverbank you would have thought she owned the place. I still couldn't deny that she was beautiful and I wanted her to be mine.

"Wanna dance?" I asked, holding out my hand.

"I don't dance with just anyone," she shouted over her shoulder as she walked away.

I watched her walk away, then spent the rest of the night trying to find her, but she was nowhere to be seen.

Later as I made my way down the road home, I found myself humming quietly as I walked. The night air was crisp in my lungs, and I felt light in my step for the first time in forever. It was cut short when I noticed my siblings sitting on the front porch.

"What are y'all doing out here?" I asked, crouching down to their level.

"Momma put the bolt on the door. She said we aren't hers and that she only has one child," my sister sniffed, "Is that true, Billy?"

"Of course not. Momma is just feeling sick again. Remember I told you sometimes she gets sick and it makes her forget things. Sit tight." I smiled and pressed a kiss to the top of each of their heads.

Carefully I made my way up the steps to the door and slammed my fist on the wooden frame. There was a soft shuffling on the other side of the door before it opened up a fraction. My mother's disheveled face peeked around the opening; her eyes lit up when she saw me.

"Hey, momma," I said softly, "why did you lock the door."

"There were people Billy. They broke in, and I had to get them out. Shoved them right outside. I have to protect the children."

"I know momma. Can you open the door? We're safe now."

"You sure, Billy?"

"Yeah, momma," I looked back at my siblings sitting on the porch, staring, "we're okay now."

She opened the door the rest of the way, and I ushered my siblings forward. As if coming out of deep fog, momma kissed both of them on the forehead and shooed them away to bed. A little while later everyone was asleep except for me. The weight of the entire night seemed to rest heavy on my shoulders as I stared into the slowly dying embers of the fireplace.

The next few days passed in a blur. Momma locked us out of the house again the next day, and it took almost two hours for her senses to clear. Every day Quincy's offer played over in my head like a broken record. On Friday while slopping the neighbor's pigs and watching my siblings trying to play with momma to no avail, I thought about what it would mean to work for Quincy. I had no idea what to expect, but I knew that things couldn't stay the same. That night I decided I would go to Trudy's and find Quincy.

Trudy's was an old bar that sat just outside the edge of town. The bar initially belonged to Trudy's husband, but after he died from drinking a bad batch of homemade moonshine, the business became hers. Her husband was a handyman by trade, so without him, the bar had begun to break down. The wood-paneled walls were riddled with termite holes, and large sections were reinforced with plywood from the old bait and tackle shop next door. Trudy herself was also a marvel.

Born Gertrude Eugene Clemens, Trudy was a massive woman. She stood nearly six feet tall, had broad shoulders, and ample buttocks you could sit a cup on. It was a trick that she used to amuse the patrons of the bar every night. The only thing small about her was her hair that she kept in a short cut afro. Trudy only wore dresses but being as large as she was there were no stores that carried her size. This fact led to Trudy's day job as a seamstress in town. What everyone loved most about Trudy was her energy. I had known of the woman my entire life and had encountered her on various occasions. Not once had I seen a frown on her face, not even at her husband's funeral.

I stepped into Trudy's, immediately feeling the weight of my problems rolling off my shoulders. Visiting Trudy's was like visiting your family. Everyone smiled and nodded to me as I made my way to the back where I knew Quincy was hiding. The smell of barbeque drifted towards me, and my mouth began to water. Trudy's brother Fred supplied the constant stream of BBQ that overflowed plates at the bars and tables. If you went around the back of the building you would see him carefully watching over the temperature of the massive makeshift smoker that he made from old barrels. Fred's real name was Ferdinand, and he was even bigger than his sister. To people he was harmless, but rumor had it that he once choked a pig with his bare hands. The smell of applewood BBQ mixed with the nauseating smell of booze as I continued through the bar. I could feel the pull of my shoes against the ever-present mixture of spilled booze and sauce that coated the floor like lacquer. As I continued searching for Quincy, I passed the dance floor where couples were pressed together dancing to the blues band playing onstage. Other couples were huddled into the darkened corners of the bar, but I couldn't make out what they were doing.

My father had always warned me about Trudy's. He would always say that the only thing that lived in a place like that was sin and death, and no matter how hard you tried to wash away your ill deeds they would cling to you like mosquitoes in July. I found Quincy sitting with his friends in the booth near the back door. The booth was a coveted spot since Fred's smoker was just outside and whoever sat there got the first pick of the meat he pulled out the smoker.

"Billy!" Quincy raised a bare rib bone in the air as I approached, "come sit and eat."

I approached carefully, my eyes darting around to the others seated at the booth. They were all unfamiliar faces to me, but all of them nodded as I sat down. Quincy slid a plate over to me, my mouth instantly watering at the sight. It had been a long time since I had the chance to eat ribs. The pigs we once owned had been sold at the market, and the neighbors never shared their meat with us. I didn't blame them, though. They had seven small mouths to feed; they didn't have enough to spare for our five. I took a small bite, trying to contain my urge to devour the pile in front of me.

"Eat, kid. I know you're hungry," Quincy laughed.

I nodded and began shoving the food into my mouth until the plate was empty. I looked down at my hands covered in sauce before wiping them on my pants.

"I want to take your offer," I said after drinking some of the water offered to me.

"How's your family? I heard your mom is getting worse."

"She's had a few bad days lately."

"And your brothers and sisters?"

"They're okay. They like reading and stuff; we're just broke." I froze as I said the words out loud for the first time.

"I can help. I have a transportation business that delivers frozen goods from town to town."

Quincy waved over a waitress, and she returned a few minutes with another place of ribs. She sat it down in front of me along with a tall glass of soda. I looked to Quincy who smiled as I launched into the new pile of food.

"What's the catch?" I asked through a mouthful of food.

"No catch," Quincy laughed, "you just transport quality frozen goods. Meat, veggies, stuff like that."

I nodded, and Quincy clapped excitedly. As I continued eating, he explained that I could begin in two days. He was the co-owner of a transportation company that he opened with his best friend. They worked with local butchers and farmers to deliver their goods from town to town. To transport the goods he would give me an ice chest to attach to the back of my bike. I ate more food and Quincy sent me home with even more.

When I arrived home, the lights were out, and my siblings were sleeping soundly. I checked in on my mother, but she wasn't in bed. I shook them awake gently, holding out the plate of food to them. They took it and began eating gratefully while I went to look for our mom. Night used to be my mom and dad's favorite time. When I was young I would always hear them talking out on the back porch. Once I snuck to the back window and watched them as they sat huddled together on the steps, looking out at the fields and talking. I knew that was where my mother would be. The sounds of night erupted around me: crickets singing melodies in harmony, the croak of frogs at the small creek hidden amongst the trees, the crackle of rats racing through the dried remains of our fields, and the snorts of the animals in pens at our neighbors settling down to rest. My mother was sitting with her head leaning against the post of the porch; her eyes focused on the non-existent crops that lay in front of her.

"We didn't have a good harvest this time, but they'll be others. Don't be sad sweetheart," she mumbled, "who is your friend out in the field?"

I looked where she pointed but only saw a blank field. When I turned back to look at her she had turned to face me where I stood in the doorway.

"Don't worry about that, man. He's taken really good care of William. William is so big and strong, but I'm worried about him. He seems so tired all the time. I wish I knew why?"

I sat down on the other side of the porch steps and watched her as she continued to ramble. She told my father about everything: the strange children in the house that day, that Hazel Jenkins put too much salt in her potato salad, and that the Harris boy got drowned in the river. After she was done talking, she just stared up at the night sky for a while. I stared upward with her, looking for the brightest stars, the ones the slaves had used to find their way to freedom. I found it shining straight above our house. A laugh involuntarily bubbled from my lips at the thought of freedom being seen at home. Mother continued to ramble on, and my eyes grew weary. I knew she wouldn't go far and would eventually fall asleep on the porch or make her way to bed. Before going inside I pressed a kiss to her cheek and mumbled I love you where only she and the crickets could hear.

Two days later I met Quincy outside the butcher shop just as the sun peeked over the valley. Together we strapped a massive chest onto the back of my bike. Once we were sure it would hold, we filled it with ice and a big frying chicken.

"Take it to this address." he handed me a folded slip of paper, "collect the money, and I'll give you your part when you get back."

I nodded and hopped onto my bike. The address on the paper was two miles away in the nicer side of Coverton. I put the paper in my pocket and pushed off headed down the road. The road was smooth beneath my tires since the path I was taking had been smoothed out to accommodate cars. The bulky framed new vehicles were all the rage. I wanted to own one someday. My father never encouraged my dream of having a car. He always called them death traps before giving me a lecture about how horses were more reliable. The irony of his way of thinking wasn't lost on me.

This time of morning ran a close second with night for my favorite time of day. Now, just like at night, I could bask in the uninterrupted beauty of nature. Dew still clung to the blades of grass stretching towards the rising sun. Storefronts sat dark, but life bustled in the back as shop owners put together their wares for the day. Trees and kudzu wound up the sides of the dilapidated buildings at the edge of the main street, attempting to reclaim the space as its own.

The few people on the street waved politely or shouted quick hellos as I passed by. Riding my bike was one of my small moments of true freedom. I had bought it with the money I made shucking peas with my mom three summers ago. It was bright blue with red handlebars, and I had secured flat pieces of aluminum from cans on the tires to make it sound like a motorbike. I laughed as I startled a few women hanging clothes on a clothesline at the house next to my destination.

"Sorry, " I shouted as I turned up the drive of a towering white house. Before I could reach up to the golden lion knocker, a man in a black tuxedo opened the door. He stared at me for a moment before shutting the door in my face. I took a step back; anger surged through my body.

As I reached up to the knocker, the door opened again to an older woman in a stained apron.

"I'm supposed to deliver a chicken to this address, " I said, feeling uncomfortable under her gaze.

"Right. Sorry about Henry." She smiled before handing me an envelope of money.

I handed her the frozen chicken, tucked the envelope in my pocket, and rode away. Halfway back to the butcher I stopped, curiosity getting the best of me. The envelope had thirty dollars in it. Shock rippled through my body. I had never seen someone pay that much for a chicken. I shoved it back into my pocket and rode back to Quincy.

When I arrived, Quincy took the money and gave me five dollars. I weighed the potential consequences of asking too much, but my curiosity won once again.

"Why did they pay so much?"

"The chickens are imported from Europe. Breed all fancy and stuff." He explained.

"Europe?" I frowned.

"Look, kid. Don't worry about it just deliver the meat and you will keep getting paid."

Despite the strange feeling I had that Quincy was keeping something from me, I continued working. Every day I would make five or six delivers to different houses around town. Most of the time it was chickens or pork butts, but on occasion it was smaller items like bags of frog legs and fish. The money was good, so I stopped asking questions. With my extra income, I bought new clothes, fixed the roof, and bought momma a comfortable chair for the back porch.

The deliveries were going off without a hitch until one day as I was making my way across town a cop pulled in front of me asking me to stop. I had never been afraid of cops, but at that moment I couldn't shake the fear that clung to me like a frightened child.

"What are you doing out this time of the morning?" The cop asked, eyeing the icebox.

"Selling fish, I caught this morning, " I lied.

He nodded for me to open the box. I obeyed showing him the fish shoved down in clear plastic bags.

"They're a little small. How much?"

"Five cents."

"I'll pass. I caught bigger ones just last week. Finish up and head home. There have been some teens causing trouble lately. I would hate for you to get mixed up with them."

I smiled and thanked him before continuing on my delivery. When I arrived back at the butcher shop, I handed Quincy the envelope and warred with myself if I should tell him about the cop.

"You okay?" Quincy asked.

I always hated moments like this when his eyes seem to bore into my soul. I had only been on the receiving end once before when a customer shorted him on a payment. My usual resolve had crumbled like the cornbread momma used to make on Sundays.

"I got stopped by a cop today."

"You're just now telling me!" Quincy yelled, slamming his fist against the table, "did he follow you? Did he look in the cooler?"

"Yeah, but I told him I was selling fish I caught this morning. He said they were tiny and let me go."

Quincy stopped for a moment and stared at me as if he was the one intimidated by me. Suddenly a smile broke out on his face, and he left to make a phone call. I strained trying to hear the conversation happening in the next room, but the only thing I could make out was my name and "street smarts". The click of the phone in the receiver echoed around the room.

"Come with me, Billy. I got something to show you." He motioned for me to follow, and I sprung to my feet.

I followed him around the counter and into the back. I had never been back there before, but I figured it was full of half butchered carcasses and ice. My assumption wasn't wrong, but Quincy kept walking into another room that held a small office. Once we were inside, he clicked the lock shut behind us and told me to sit. He sat on the edge of the desk for a moment staring at me. I did my best not to flinch under his scrutiny.

"You have been delivering more than just frozen goods." He began, "each of those animals you've delivered had opium inside of them."

"That's gross, " I frowned thinking of someone smoking a pipe full of fish guts.

"We wrap the drugs up nice and tight before they go in. That's why those deliveries make so much money."

"Okay?" I was still confused.

"Look, Billy. I got drafted, and I'm going to be leaving soon, and I end someone to take over while I'm gone—or if I don't come back."

"What about the others? Rob? Mike?"

"They're good guys, but they're dumb and can't think on their feet. But you. You can think fast and go unnoticed. There's something about you that people trust. I need someone I can trust to take over."

“I'll think about it.”

When I arrived home, momma was sitting in her chair on the back porch. Tears raced down her cheeks, and she scrubbed at them angrily when she saw me. I knew from the look in her eyes that now was one of her moments of lucidity. The steps creaked underneath me as I sat down in front of her. She placed a hand on my head, her skin warm to the touch.

"I'm so sorry, Billy. I failed you. I failed all of you. I'm so weak. Your father kept me strong." She wiped tears again.

I leaned my head to rest on her knees as she patted my head. I could hear the hitch in her breath as she tried to calm down.

"You need a father figure to show you the right way. How did you get this chair and those clothes?"

"Do you want to cook dinner with me, momma?"

"This chair wasn't here before. Where? Did they bring it?"

"Momma?" I sat up watching as her gaze faded and began darting around the porch.

"Tell them to leave me alone. They won't leave," she cried.

I pretended to shoo away people from the porch. The neighbors watched from their stoop, and I smiled, nodding that everything was okay. An hour later I got momma tucked into bed and quieter. She was still mumbling about the people who came to visit on the porch, even as she drifted off into sleep. My brothers and sister went to sleep soon after. I stayed awake listening to the symphony of crickets give way to the chorus of morning birds. By the time the rest of the town was up, and bustling about I had accepted Quincy's offer.

Quincy was shipped off to war a week after I accepted his offer. The neighborhood began to break down as more and more young men were shipped off to war as well. Just as quickly as they were gone, they returned a year later when the war ended. Some of them returned with fresh scars, still scabbed over from the trenches and buzzed heads that the ladies loved. Others returned with missing limbs and headaches only appeased by the opium that I supplied. Then there were those that returned in mahogany boxes covered with a flag, flowers, freshly spilled tears, and pleas that fell on deaf ears. All of them returned with dreams. Dreams about the war and what they did. Dreams about the men they left behind. Dreams about the men they were before, and nightmares about the men they were becoming.

They never told any stories about the dark parts of war, except when they were so doped up on opium that the truth came spilling out from their lips. The stories they told were of the fun times. Tales of shore leave, exotic liquor, and even more exotic women. Quincy came back with similar stories and was just as ecstatic that business was booming. Marla still hated my guts, but there were plenty of other women who loved me and the perks that came along with dating me. I spent my free time learning guitar and crooning with A. W. Even though he didn't tell his son the truth, A.W confessed to me that he missed Quincy every day he was gone and was afraid that his son wouldn't return. Over the year A. W had become like a father to me. He told me stories from Quincy's childhood. When Quincy was little he looked up to A.W until he saw him interacting with the other former slaves. He had found out that day that his father had been the last slave to leave the plantation. Since that day Quincy had called him a coward. A. W tried to explain that he told people that he stayed to make sure all the other slaves had left for good. Even the owner abandoned the plantation before A.W since his business went under.

"I tried to tell myself that I was protectin' others, but the truth is Billy...I'm 'fraid of change. All my life was 'bout around my work and keeping folks safe," A.W said taking a long swig of the flask in his hand, "When we were free, they ain't need me for that no mo'. What was I 'posed to do? I get why he hates me."

With Quincy back home, I tried to step down. Instead, he agreed to run the business together. Running the business with him was difficult. Since he got back from war, he was angrier. His once calm and thoughtful demeanor had given way to ruthlessness. The year he came home, we all attended Blue River together. Everything was going fine until a man bumped into Quincy's shoulder. Without hesitation, Quincy headbutted him and began raining down punches. By the time we were able to pull them apart, the man's face was an indistinguishable mess. His constant drinking fueled Quincy's anger and caused the rift between him and A.W to develop further.

The years continued to tick by, and things got worse. My mother's mind faded more with each passing day, and the doctors encouraged me to send her to an asylum. I refused every time because of the stories I heard. Stories of straight jackets and orderlies that suffocated patients. Stories of lobotomies done while the patients were still awake, their screams bouncing off the walls that had already seen countless horrors. Stories of darkened hallways and corners where even a sane person would come face to face with their demons.

I did the best I could to help Quincy too. Too often, my help consisted of picking him up from Trudy's just to make sure he passed out in his own bed. A.W got sick as well, and his health declined rapidly. Some days it was impossible for him to move at all. On days like that, I would carry him to the porch and sit him in the chair while I played guitar. During his moments of lucidity he would hum along to my plucking or sing mumbled words that I pieced together later.

The reaper think he funny.

Think it's funny to make me wait.

He stand in every corner now.

Wit' that smile on his face.

I ain't got nothin' to hang on to.

I got nothin' to make me stay.

So reaper,

Come on reaper,

Come on reaper,

Don't make me wait.

It was one of the days on the porch with A.W that Marla began to take an interest in me. I was in the middle of restringing A.W prized guitar when she asked to take a seat on the step.

"Can I help you, Ms. Marla?" I said, trying to keep my voice even despite the pounding in my chest.

"I wanted to apologize. I thought you were full of yourself."

"What gave you that notion?"

"The way you grabbed my arm that night at the river. You made it seem like I owed you my time."

"Well, I apologize ma'am. That was never my intent."

"My daddy also told me to stay away from you. He said that you just wanted me for my money, but I know that's not true now. My daddy's been gone a year now, and I find myself longing for some company."

"I appreciate you coming by Ms. Marla, and I accept your apology."

She smiled, and it felt like every song that had been locked up in my heart all these years came bursting forth with newfound passion.

"Would you like to go out with me Marla St. Troy?"

She agreed, and two nights later, we found ourselves on the dance floor at Trudy's. Our courtship was better than I had imagined. We spent countless days driving through the neighborhood and nights on weekend getaways. My brother and sister where ten now, so I let them fend for themselves on the days I was gone. They took a more significant role taking care of momma and A.W while I was gone. Some nights Marla and I would make our way to the river and sit at its bank. It seemed like a completely different place without the festival. It was a peaceful backdrop for the chaos of the dwindling opium trade. One day as we sat along the bank Marla told me about her father.

Julian St. Troy had been a house slave all his life, so when slavery ended he saw it as a chance to run things instead of taking orders. He had taken the job as a mayoral assistant in the hopes of using it to move up. It was too little too late when he realized he was still a slave but with a different title. Marla's mother had died when she was little. The only thing she remembered about the woman came from flashes of memory about ribbons in her hair and glasses of ice-cold tea on the porch.

"Life has got to mean more than this town," she sighed, "that's what my daddy always said."

"Sounds like your daddy was as big of a dreamer as mine."

"Ain't nothing wrong with dreaming Billy. Don't be so blue."

I laughed, "Billy Blue. That ain't half bad."

We talked all through the night, but every time Marla asked me about work, I would change the subject. All she needed to know was that I worked with deliveries.

In 1920 Prohibition hit full force across the nation, and the opium business began to fade in favor of moonshine. The new mayor even shut down Trudy's. It took a little convincing, but Quincy agreed that we had to get in on the ground floor of the bootlegging business. My hunch paid off, and business was booming once more. Quincy handled making the shine, and I handled transporting it to speakeasies in the area. After her persistent questions about my job I finally admitted to Marla that I was a bootlegger. To my surprise she asked to help with the money since she was good with numbers.

A year later, the business was great, but A.W health continued to fail. Early on an oddly chilly morning in July, we found A.W out on the porch, Maggie in hand, and not a breath in his body. We buried him with the guitar on a bright Sunday afternoon. Quincy stood stoic the entire time but broke down into tears later that night as I dragged him out of one of the neighborhood speakeasies.

In August of the same year, I made Marleen Olivia St. Troy, my wife. The death of A.W had cast a shadow of sadness over our lives, and we hoped the wedding would help get rid of the gray. We spared no expense and invited the entire town. All of the men, women, and children I met at Blue River came into town to join in the festivities. Fred set up his smoker for us, and of course there was plenty of shine to go around.

"Marleen Olivia St. Troy when you stepped into my life I thought I had it all figured out. You weren't wrong when you said that I was full of myself. When I was younger, I thought that life had dealt me a bad hand and there was no point of wanting anything bigger. Then you showed me that even if a hand is bad a few good cards can make all the difference."

After the wedding, we moved into a big house at the edge of town. Living in a place like that would have been impossible if it were anywhere but Coverton. We moved everyone in with us, but I tried to get my siblings to push for more. I wanted them to break out of this town and use the stuff they learned in school. They weren't like me. They were good at learning things. Momma just sat and stared so I put a big window with a seat that overlooked the pond. Marla took care of her during the day, and I would sing to her at night. Business was going well, and we expanded to send our shine across the state. I thought I was finally happy until August 22, 1926 when I held my son, Jefferson Ambrose Scheets in my arms for the first time. Holding him in my arms, let me know what true happiness felt like. Marla would tease me that I was lucky he only got my bright smile and dark brown eyes. Around the same time Quincy's drinking became a problem.

After weeks of being short on product we realized that it was Quincy drinking the shine before it could be delivered. He stopped for a short time then started again. Amidst Quincy's decline momma died in October of 1927. She had gone missing late into the evening. We searched for her around the pond, and the shops she once visited. When we finally found her she was huddled next to dad's grave. Her head rested against the tombstone, and there was a small smile on her face.

It seemed like when momma died the town died with her. People moved away to the city for work. The fields died. Stores shut down. Marla had made sure we saved money over the years, so we stayed in town. Quincy continued drinking heavily and began to suffer from PTSD. Whenever a car fired off, or a gun popped he would drop to the ground and began yelling commands to soldiers that we're only ghosts in his head. Once when I returned from a supply run I found him sitting at the kitchen table, a tear-stained note bleeding ink on the white table cloth, and a shotgun ready to be fired clutched between his lips. Upon seeing me, he broke down in tears and begged me to make the ghosts go away. I found him some help in the form of a farm in a neighboring town. The farm helped Quincy quit drinking, but he turned to opium instead. Despite the drug use he seemed level headed and began to act like his old self.

Three years later, he had kicked the opium habit and began a family of his own. My family expanded in the Spring of 1930 when we welcomed home my daughter Collette Penelope Scheets, but we called her Penny on account of her being so small when she was born. The business expanded to Alabama, where the demand for moonshine was still high. With the newly boosted income, we went on vacations as a family and good times seemed to be on the rise. Without warning, Marla began to grow distant. We rarely walked the neighborhood together anymore, and the nights we spent staring up at the stars faded into memory.

During the summer of 1933, a week before my son's birthday, I found myself drawn to the river. To my surprise, people were setting up for the festival. There hadn't been a proper Blue River festival in two years. I found out that they had all decided to host the festival in honor of A.W and hopefully boost the ever dying spirits of the townsfolk. Filled with excitement I went to find Quincy and the rest of the boys so we could help pitch tents.

After hours of setting up tents and fire pits, I took a break. I made my way down the river's edge, following it as it churned angrily in its banks. My gaze was transfixed on the raging water when the sound of a gun clicked behind me. I turned to see Quincy pointing a pistol at my head, his eyes wet with tears.

"You been stealing from us. We're down ten bottles, and you were the last one with it, " he hissed.

"I would never steal."

"Don't lie to me!" He stepped closer as I stepped back.

Two of our men came around the bend and raced to help me, but Quincy turned and fired into the dirt at their feet. When he stepped closer, I could smell the moonshine on his breath, and see the glazed over look in his eyes from smoking. I punched him hard in the jaw making him stagger backward enough for me to grab at the gun.

"Tell the truth!" I screamed, trying to wrench the gun from his hands.

A rage-filled scream ripped from Quincy's throat as he shoved me off of him. I stumbled backward toward the bank, and I felt the dirt give way under my weight as I slipped into the water. A hand shot forward and pulled my head above water even as the river raged around me, begging to pull me under. My eyes met Quincy's as he shouted for the men to get help. When he turned back to me his eyes did not reflect the fear in mine. Instead of fear or anger there was only sadness. Even the river seemed to go silent for a moment as he let go of my hand and I slipped beneath the water once more. The current pulled me downriver, tiring out my body as I tried to get to the surface. I surfaced once and heard the faint cries of my name upstream, but I was dragged under before I could scream for help. Water flooded down my throat as I lost against my body's instincts. It felt like fire, ripping and tearing at my insides. My body gave up, and I felt myself sinking, but as I sank I became aware of the silence. The silence that I had basked in so many times now seemed deafening. I sank until the silence gave way to darkness.

I found out in a later life that they had covered my death by saying the bridge broke as I stood looking over the water. Two weeks after they found my body caught in some trees roots downstream, they tore down the "broken bridge" and replaced it with a large covered one. Quincy had died in a bar fight a year later encouraged by too much moonshine and heroin. With both of us gone the business went under, and our wives turned to odd jobs mending clothes to keep the rumors of their wealth at bay. My son joined the Army but died a year before he would have come home. Collette opened her own tailor shop and called it Collette's Custom Clothier, but everyone called it Collette's. I had to learn about my family's fate from newspaper clippings.

I realized that A.W was right. Dead men dream. He left out that they are always nightmares.

Ice rattled in the glass as Rose sat it down on the counter. She took the notebook and flipped through it again, stopping on the picture of the deer.

“What’s the deer mean?” Rose questioned.

“I’ve seen that name before.” I frowned as I pulled out my phone.

When I googled Collette’s a shop in Coverton was the first result. I vaguely remembered the tailor shop in the middle of town. It had expanded over the years to include the antique store next door. A distant memory of going in the store with my mother sprang to mind. I believe we went there to get a suit tailored for my father.

“That’s freaky. Look up the name,” Rose said, looking over my shoulder at my phone.

A search of William Scheets brought up an article done years ago in Coverton about a famous local bootlegger. The facts of the article were the same things we had just read in my aunt's notebook. I could feel my palms breaking out in a nervous sweat as I read about his death from falling into the Blue River. The original purpose of the article was to shine a light on the origin of the nickname of the covered bridge. A cold chill raced down my spine as I read, my heart pounded against the skeleton cage of my chest as if trying to escape.

"How is all of it true? She knew all of the details? Did she just do a bunch of research? What's the point if she did? Why would she?" I felt myself spiraling, but couldn't stop myself from hyperventilating.

The thud of a shot glass on the booth's table startled me and redirected my focus. I looked up at Rose, who was smirking as she knocked back the other shot on the table and slid one over to me. I took the shot, hissing as the whiskey burned on the way down.

"What do you want all of it to mean?" Rose asked.

"I don't know. I try and stay out of stuff."

"Look. I came here to drink and maybe play some pool. This," she said, pointing to the journal, "this is way more interesting."

"You have a weird definition of interesting."

"Hot chick. Booze. A great story. Sounds like a good time to me."

I dissolved into laughter, but I wasn't sure if it was from the liquor of the absurdity of the situation. I leaned back against the booth, closing my eyes and focusing on my breathing. Rose leaned back as well and tilted her head up towards the ceiling. I'm not sure what came over me, but I took out the previous two notebooks I had read and set them in front of her. She quirked an eyebrow at me for a moment before smiling and picking up the first book. The note from my aunt toppled out onto the table. Creases ran across the page from the countless times I had folded and unfolded the paper. I nodded, giving her permission to read it. Once she was done, she set the paper on the table and let out a long slow breath.

"That's some heavy stuff, Ky," she sighed."

Rose waved to the bartender, and he showed up a moment later with two more shots of whiskey. Once he was gone, she lifted her shot in the air, and I did the same.

"To wherever this takes us."

After we knocked back the shots, I leaned against the wall next to me and watched as she read the other two notebooks. Her brow was furrowed in a mixture of concentration and what I am sure was confusion. As I watched her read, it felt like a weight had been lifted off of my shoulders. Before I knew it, I had dozed off and was only awakened by Rose's hand on my shoulder.

"Ky, wake up," she whispered, "I'm in."

"What? In what?" I groaned, rubbing my eyes.

The short nap had been the most restful sleep I had in a long time. Rose was smiling as she showed me the notes she had taken as she read the other notebooks. I took a look at them as she explained that she was trying to crossreference the genus and species of the spider and fly Sheryl had written about with the life cycle she described.

"I'm not sure what all of this is, but I'm in either way."

We spent another hour fact-checking the information in the journals before going our separate ways. Rose wrote her number down on a napkin instead of just putting it into my phone like a normal person.

She said that when it came to some matters she liked the flair of tradition.

When I arrived home, the condo was dark save for a single light coming from my mother's bedroom. Silently I made my way into her room and turned off the light before going to my room. I tucked the notebooks into the safety of the drawer underneath my bed and snuggled into my covers. I'm not sure if it was the liquor or the satisfaction of sharing my struggles with someone who believed me, but that night, I fell asleep and dreamed of nothing.

13

Dried leaves crumbled underneath my feet as I crashed through the treeline. My breath came out in heavy pants that billowed out like fog in front of my face as I ran. I shifted to keep the shadowy figure in my peripheral. Suddenly the figure darted ahead of me and was lost in the tree line. At that same moment, I burst forward into a clearing. Time seemed to slow as I paused to take in my surroundings. The figure was nowhere to be seen. I closed my eyes and slowed my breathing as Rose had taught me. The forest around me teemed with life and one by one I filtered out its sounds. First the birds screeching overhead. Next the skitter of squirrels and chipmunks through the dead leaves. The low whistle of the wind making its way through the trees. There. A footstep. Careful and measured. Close. Before I could move out of the way I felt the poke of something into my back. Just as quickly an arm wrapped around my neck, squeezing slightly.

"The Children of Demeter require your blood," Rose hissed.

I snorted with laughter as she doubled over in laughter as well. She tossed the stick in her hand off to the side and sat down on the grass. The grass was a cool relief to my heated skin as I lay back on the grass next to her. The only sound in the clearing for a moment were the two of us slowing our breathing to bring our heart rates down after the run.

"Running from murderers is exhausting," Rose panted.

"No one has chased me for months, Rose." I rolled my eyes, "Do you think it's weird how they just left me alone?"

"Better knock on wood," Rose teased.

“Pick a tree.”

“You know Ky. Most people would be happy not being chased by a murderous cult.”

I shrugged and turned my head to look around the clearing. At the edge of the clearing near a sawed-off tree stump, there was a line of daffodils growing.

“They’re beautiful, right,” I said, pointing to the flowers.

“Genus Narcissus. They are a symbol of spring and rebirth or self-love,” Rose added.

“Self-love. More like narcissism,” I snorted.

“Do you know the story of Narcissus?”

“No. I don’t think we read that one yet,” I said, trying to remember the name from the research we had been doing on Greek myths.

Rose stood, grabbed one of the daffodils, then laid down on the ground next to me, and held the flower up to the sunlight.

Narcissus was a hunter renown for his beauty. When he was young, his mother was given a prophecy that the boy would live a long life as long as "he never knows himself". During his life he was pursued by men and women alike. The most famous of his male suitors was Aminias who upon Narcissus rejecting him killed himself on Narcissus' doorstep while praying to the gods to teach Narcissus a lesson. His most famous female suitor was Echo, a nymph who was cursed by Hera after keeping her from catching Zeus in his infidelity. Hera cursed her only to repeat the last thing she hears. The gods favored Narcissus for his strength and physique, but the prophecy given to his mother at his birth was out of their control. One day while on a hunt, Narcissus decided to rest near a pool of water.

As he sat along the water's edge, he looked over and saw the most beautiful person he had ever encountered. Of course he fell madly in love. Not knowing it was his reflection he reached into the water to touch his newfound love, but when his fingers touched the water his lover vanished. He tried over and over to reach out to the beautiful figure in the water but could not touch them. Even though he couldn't touch his lover, he refused to leave their side. From there the story varies a little. Some say he died of starvation as he refused to leave the water's edge. Others say he stabbed himself in sorrow at being rejected. Then some believe he reached into the water one last time and drowned in its depths. What remains true in all the stories is that Narcissus died at the edge of the water and it was said that in the Underworld he stayed by the river Styx where he could still see his love in the water.

"After that, Narcissus became a symbol of obsession. Self-love isn't dangerous, but self-obsession is dangerous. But it's not just self. When you become blinded by devotion to anything it's dangerous. You become so consumed by the idea of perfection that anything less than that is unworthy," Rose said, plucking the petals off the daffodil in her hand, "the prophecy said that he couldn't know himself, but the true issue is that to know himself was to know perfection or what others created as the idea of perfection."

"How do you know all of this?" I wondered as I watched the petals being swept up by the wind.

"My uncle was a history professor. When I would stay with him, he read me myths instead of bedtime stories."

"Why haven't you told me about him before?"

"I...I don't really like talking about him. He died a while back when I was in high school. He was killed in a head-on collision." She swallowed hard.

"I'm so sorry."

"How's your mom? Is she still being weird?" Rose asked, clearing her throat.

I sighed and scrubbed my hand over my face. My mother had been acting odd still. She was constantly bringing Trent around. A fact that bothered me immensely. The last thing I wanted to see when I returned home was my ex on the couch.

"Are you trying to date him?" Rose quirked an eyebrow.

"Absolutely not. That chapter is done. He's...obsessive."

We stayed in the clearing for a little longer before making our way back to our cars and then to my condo. A groan pulled past my lips when I opened the door to see Travis and my mother on the couch together. Rose stopped in the doorway, her jaw clenched as she and Trent made eye contact. The two hated each other since they had met at my condo a month ago. It was hard to explain where the hatred came from, but every encounter between them ended in an argument.

"I should go," Rose said, patting my shoulder.

"No. This is my condo," I said, turning to look at Trent, "I need you to leave."

"He's not causing any harm, Ky," my mother frowned.

"I don't want him here."

"He's my guest."

"It's my condo."

"I'll go," Trent interjected, "it's no trouble."

Trent leaned down and pressed a kiss to my mom's forehead before excusing himself. On his way out the door, he bumped Rose's shoulder, and I was surprised she didn't punch him. Once he was gone, my mom turned her nose up at Rose and went into her room, slamming the door. I rolled my eyes and flopped down on my couch next to Rose. She tucked her feet underneath herself and began flipping through the channels. The hodgepodge sound of the channels filled the silence of the room.

"So…what about book four. Have you read it yet?" Rose asked.

Over the past month, we had read and reread the previous books. All of the information in them checked out, and I was beginning to believe there was some validity to what they said. We had also done research on the Children of Persephone and Demeter. The names of the opposing cults were the only useful piece of information Trent had given me.

"Those books are nothing but trouble, and Miriam was no help when I called her," I huffed remembering the pointless conversation with Miriam a few weeks ago.

When I asked her to tell me the story of the beginnings of the cult she first became angry that I called it a cult, and then said I had to prove I believed in the cause before she would tell me anything further. I asked what I needed to do, to which she replied if I had to ask I wasn't ready. For the past month I had not encountered any unusual people tailing me or been attacked, and I wanted it to stay that way even though my curiosity had been piqued. In particular delving into William "Billy Blue" Scheets had proved an adventure. We found more newspaper articles that called him a community partner, a philanthropist, and a pillar in the Coverton community. I found it odd that I had never heard of him while growing up, but when I mentioned the name to my mother it caused an argument and an hour-long rant about the wages of sin. We spent the hours until sundown watching T.V and talking. It was a routine that we had fallen into over the past month.

Rose had quickly become a friend and confidant of mine. She was one of the few people that knew the secrets I held, and I trusted her more than anyone else. Sometimes we would discuss details over dinner or drinks, but I couldn't shake the guilt that sat heavy in my gut as we found out more about the cult. From what we discovered, the cults were mortal enemies and had waged war with each other for centuries. It was nearly impossible to decide who the good guys were since both sides were responsible for numerous deaths. Their members included people from all sectors: politicians, doctors, professors. The issue with all the information was that it all came from conspiracy sites, nestled alongside articles on Bigfoot sightings. One fact, in particular, stood out among all of them. According to the sites, the Children of Demeter were represented by a golden torch. Its flame represented Demeter's search for her daughter and their never-ending commitment to their cause. The flame was so engrained in their being that true believer's eyes would sometimes glow gold.

We went over our notes for a few more hours, before Rose left with the promise of returning tomorrow afternoon. My mother was still holed up in her room, and not even the temptation of takeout from her favorite restaurant could get her to come out. I gave up on trying to get her to come out of her room and stretched out on the sofa. Day gave way to night, and I found myself dozing before falling fully asleep. I began to awake when I felt as if I were being watched. A soft shuffling filled my ears, and first I ignored it, thinking it was mom getting a glass of water, or sneaking to eat the box of fried chicken I had bought her for dinner. However, the shuffling got louder as whatever was making the sound drew closer. Ice spread through my veins and the hair of my arm prickled. Slowly I opened my eyes to find my mother standing next to the couch, her eyes were closed, and she was mumbling under her breath.

"Mom?" I croaked.

The mumbling stopped, and her head lifted to focus on me.

Golden eyes stared back in the darkness.

###

Made in the USA
Monee, IL
07 March 2020